THEIR JUST DESERTS

Freshwater Bay Novel Series

Nell Grey

CONTENTS

ABOUT NELL GREY

DON'T MISS OUT

Sign up to Nell Grey's newsletter for news about Nell Grey's novels, plus access to some great book offers.

Bonus: follow me on Goodreads and Amazon

If you like reading my books, please help spread the word about them by leaving an honest review.

Hearing your thoughts about my stories makes my day.

Hope you enjoy this story as much as I loved writing it.

Nell xx

BOOKS BY NELL GREY

The Freshwater Bay Series:

The Strictly Business Proposal - Gareth and Beth

The Actor's Deceit - Rhys and Ariana

Their Just Deserts - Owen and Alys

The Rural Escape - Madog and Jo

Trust Me Find Me Series:

★ ★ ★ ★ ★

A SPELLBINDING DRAMA THAT WILL HAVE YOU ENTHRALLED

Trust Me

Find Me

CHAPTER 1

---------*---------

"**D**ance with me."

Owen Morgan, professional rugby star, and what Alys Edwards classed as an Adonis of a man, was holding out his hand.

To her. A humble pastry chef with a wobbly arse and flabby thighs.

And, boy; did he look hot.

She gazed up at his tanned, rugby-rugged face and those piercing blue eyes of his that were now bearing down directly upon her.

"No. You've got a girlfriend."

He didn't deny it or try to explain Julia away. He couldn't. She'd been with him all day. Until she'd slumped off on her own to bed.

"It's you I'm gonna marry, Alys Edwards."

He chased that up with a dazzling smile.

"When I first tasted that chocolate dessert of yours, I told my brothers you're *the one*."

Alys screwed her nose. He was full of it.

"That's because I lace my chocolate mousse gateau with a secret love drug... And right now, I'd say you're trippin', pal."

The six-foot-five man-mountain continued to tower over her. He was not taking no for an answer.

"You can't help it," she rambled on under his magnetic gaze. "You're doped up to your eyeballs. Totally under my powers. In fact, you're the tenth proposal I've had this evening."

"Come on, Alys. Take a risk. It's Van Morrison."

He dropped her another sizzling smile that made her heart thump and won him that dance.

"What's the worst that could happen?" he coaxed as he led her outside onto the dancefloor by the side of the wedding marquee.

"That I get my eyes scratched out by your girlfriend?"

"I'd protect you," he whispered into her ear, sending goosebumps right through her.

So there she was, in spite of her protestations, with Owen *Greek-god* Morgan swaying to Van Morrison's Moondance beneath the cover of October skies. This had to be full-moon madness.

She gasped as Owen's huge arms caged her even more closely. Pressing her against his vast muscular torso and feeling the base of her back, his hands dropped down glossing over the ample curves of her buttocks.

Her palms that she'd tried so hard to fix chastely on his chest, now wandered up around his neck.

Bending his head down towards her shoulder, she felt his hot breath lingering on her collarbone. It moved deliciously along her neck and then gently upwards until she felt his mouth sweeping softly over her, delicately tasting her lips.

She really did try her very best to resist his charms. But as his mouth covered hers, she opened and deepened their kiss, aiding and abetting in it becoming a hot tangle of all kinds of wrong.

The music ended and so did the kiss.

Abruptly.

A sharp slap stung Owen Morgan's cheek.

"I think your girlfriend's keeping your bed warm."

Alys rubbed her smarting hand.

"One woman in his bed and another on the dancefloor," she huffed out loud as she stomped away. "Owen Morgan, who do you think you are?" And more importantly, who did he think she was?

They both knew she'd been a willing accomplice.

Still grumbling to herself, she went to check that the catering team had finished their clean-down. When she'd agreed to help her friend Rhys with the food for his wedding, she hadn't expected to hook up with his brother. The Best Man.

She prayed that no one had posted up a photo of them. A barrage of accusations was the last thing she needed when she got back to Paris from her weekend in Wales.

"What did I do wrong?" Owen asked his eldest brother, rubbing his face.

He was coming off the dance floor with his wife, Beth. Alys' best friend.

Gareth sniggered, "You're the Doctor of Psychology. You work it out."

Owen was one of the last to leave the marquee. He'd hung around drinking away the last dregs of the night, long after Alys had gone home. Talking bullshit with a couple of cousins and an old school friend, hoping that if he stayed out long enough Julia would be sound asleep.

It was a little after three by the time Owen opened the bedroom door, swearing under his breath as he tripped over Julia's stilettos in the dark.

He'd been trying his best to keep as quiet as he could so as not to wake her, but the stairs, the floorboards, everything in this old farmhouse creaked under his heavy drunken footsteps.

He needn't have bothered being stealthy. The light snapped on as soon as he reached the bed.

His heart sank. Julia, dressed in a black lace negligee, lay in wait for him on top of the covers. Awake and ready to pounce.

After she'd seen the invite on his fridge door, there'd been no way of not inviting her. A weak moment he now regretted.

"Where've you been? I've been waiting for you for hours."

Owen shrugged.

"With my brothers."

Slumping down onto the bed, he began pulling his shoes and socks off. Turning his back on Julia, he unbuttoned his shirt.

She felt his involuntary flinch as her fingers ran along his bare back. He wasn't feeling it. Not with her.

"Julia, it's been a long day."

He quickly pulled the t-shirt over his chest and she slank away.

"Suit yourself. I'm not begging."

She slipped huffily under the covers as he exchanged his trousers for a pair of boxers.

He could tell that more was brewing. The woman had one hell of a temper. He hoped she'd save it for the morning when his head was clearer. When he could let her down gently somewhere more private than his parents' house. A walk on the beach.

He felt her heavy breathing as he got under the duvet.

"What were you doing dissing me like that in front of your mother?"

She tugged the quilt possessively around her.

"What the...? Shush! Julia, they'll hear you," he whispered a little too loudly.

His parents were a couple of bedrooms down the hall. He knew from experience that the sound in the old farmhouse carried.

"I don't care if I wake the whole house. You didn't need to embarrass me like that."

"Like what?"

Like, by kissing Alys? Had she seen them?

"Like, telling your mother that we're never getting married."

"Oh that... Well, we're not."

Rolling to face him, her lips were pursed tight. Her stare was angry and more than a little scary.

He rubbed his eyes, trying to settle himself to sleep.

"When are you gonna start treating me properly, and commit to me as a girlfriend?"

He yawned. He was too drunk to deal with this.

"You agreed too, remember. No-strings-attached. *Your words*, Julia."

"Yeah, well, I've been pulling your string for over a year now. We're way beyond booty calls."

He stretched over her head with his arm and hit the light switch, then patted the top of her head with his huge hand.

"Look, it's gonna be tricky for me over the next few months, now get some sleep. Good night."

He closed his eyes again. The diaphanous image of Alys floated around his head. And after tonight, he now knew the feel of her too. The curve of her back. And her voluptuous bottom. How her ample breasts felt as they'd been pressed up against him. The softness of her lips on his.

"I can't believe you did that," she snapped at him in the darkness, popping his dream of Alys like a soap bubble.

His head was starting to pound, and it wasn't from the drink.

"Eh?"

"Paris. What on earth made you sign? A whole year and you never even asked me. I'm on the sofa of the UK's number one talk show, Owen. I'm presenting the sports news on prime time. These gigs don't fall from the sky. I need you with me in London, not in bloody Paris."

He knew exactly why she wanted him there. He'd be Julia's accessory. On her arm like a designer handbag. The sports-star boyfriend at glitzy parties. Martinis with media lovies. Delivering a winning smile and a witty line.

"Julia, I can't commit to a relationship."

She huffed, pulling the covers around her head as Owen rolled onto his side, his back to her. Finally getting some peace to sleep.

Under the circumstances, he wouldn't tell her about the deal he'd done that week. How he'd invested a large chunk of his hard-won sports star earnings buying The Lobster Pot Inn, a rundown hotel in the harbour.

Best not to tell her either that he'd also bought the nearby boathouse off Gareth and Beth. A place to live after his rugby career ended.

Yes, he was off to Paris for a few months, but his home and his future business interests were here. In West Wales. In Freshwater Bay.

Whether Julia liked it or not.

"Saw you getting on very well with a certain rugby player last night."

Beth shot a mischievous grin at her best mate. It was Sunday morning and Alys had been staying with them at the boathouse over the wedding weekend.

Just into October, the weather was still warm enough to sit out. And they were enjoying the sea air at the outside table on the boathouse deck. Beth had made them all scrambled eggs and toast. And her husband Gareth, Owen's brother, was feeding their son Finn in the highchair inside. Giving them a little girl time.

Alys took a sip of her freshly squeezed orange juice.

"Owen was a bit drunk last night. He got a little bit carried away."

Beth milled black pepper over her eggs.

"He's into you."

Alys very much doubted that. Not with her fat arse and thunder thighs.

"Take it from me," Beth continued, nodding towards Alys' ample chest. "I was watching. And that boy was appreciating your assets for most of the wedding."

Alys giggled.

"No! Don't be daft."

"Not with his glamorous TV girlfriend there, too."

"I'm not joking. He couldn't keep his eyes off you. I'm not sure what's going on with Julia Johnson. Owen's told Gareth that it's an open arrangement. A friends with benefits type thing. But from what Julia was hinting at last night, she's not got the memo on that one."

Alys finished her eggs.

"He'll get his just deserts with her, I'm sure. Guys like him, it's all about the chase. Once they win the woman, it's game over. Move on to the next one."

Beth didn't disagree.

"I saw that slap you gave him. That musta hurt."

Alys chewed her lip.

"Oh well. At least I left my mark on him, eh?"

She hoped he'd forgive her. He was a tough boy; he must have worse than that every Saturday on the rugby pitch.

They chatted about Freshwater Bay and their friends. Alys and Beth had worked together as chefs in London until Beth met Gareth Morgan, an architect. She'd left London to run a restaurant she'd inherited on the Welsh coast.

Alys had helped her out a few months before, when Finn was born. And she'd been working there the night Beth's restaurant, La Galloise, was burned down.

"What's the latest from the police?" Alys asked.

Beth's eyes drifted across the water to the clifftop above. A couple of bulldozers now sat where her beautiful restaurant had once stood.

"The arson charge wouldn't stick, but they got the guy on drug charges. He's in prison again on a seven stretch."

That was a relief. Alys had been upstairs asleep when the fire took hold. Gareth's brother Rhys, the groom at the wedding, had saved her that night. They'd been firm friends ever since.

Rhys bore the burns, but Alys had scars too. Invisible ones that haunted her every couple of weeks. Waking her up screaming, covered in sweat.

She leaned back in her seat and took a deep breath. Even thinking about them was terrifying.

"Life goes on."

Unconsciously, Beth touched her belly.

"That it does."

It was still a big secret and an even bigger surprise, but she'd whispered to Alys that baby number two was on its way.

The waves lapped gently against the deck. Designed by Gareth, the boathouse was a Scandinavian style open-plan house. An architect's dream. The eco-chalet had wall to wall glass and dramatic views of the sea. The wrap-around deck sat above the water and there was a jetty at the front slipping into the sea.

The place was one huge toddler hazard.

"How are you going to cope now that Finn's moving around?"

"Gareth's been super-busy."

"I'll say," Alys smirked.

Beth coloured up.

"No! Cheeky. Busy with the building plans. Our new restaurant. Rhys' farmhouse renovation... And building our new family home."

Alys raised an eyebrow.

"But, you love it here?"

"We're gonna need more space. And a garden. Somewhere for Finn to play. We've sold it already."

No one was more organised or focussed than Beth.

"Have you thought more about coming back and working with us? Please say you will. You're my wing-woman."

Alys was a part of Beth's grand schemes too. She squinted in the sunlight as she stared out to sea.

"You've got everything covered for now, though?"

"Well, yes, while we're rebuilding the restaurant. But after that, The Lobster Pot will be a blank canvas. And there's a new owner who's up for fresh ideas. We could run it together as a hotel? It'd be like old times, again. Me and you. What d'ya say?"

She didn't want to disappoint her friend, but things had changed.

"Beth, I'm not sure. I've met someone. In Paris. His name's Leo. He's French."

CHAPTER 2

---------*---------

Paul Campbell was packing away the plastic boxes with the last of the kitchen equipment to take back to The Lobster Pot.

Catering for the wedding had been fun. Working up the dishes with Alys. Being out there, serving the guests, instead of being holed up in a hot kitchen.

Renting The Lobster Pot had been an adequate stopgap whilst La Galloise was being rebuilt. But as Beth's deputy, he was looking forward to getting back to running a smart French restaurant again. Their loyal customers had moved with them, but it wasn't the same. The Lobster Pot had seen better days.

"Hey, Paul."

A tall, athletic-looking woman in a tight pair of jeans and a summery sleeveless shirt was making her way towards him.

They'd met last night. She was the owner of the wedding marquee business and she'd left him her card, asking him if he'd like to do some weddings catering for her, on the fly. He wasn't interested. He was busy enough as it was.

Desperately scouring his mind, he took a punt.

"Hi, Fiona."

She frowned.

"Vanessa."

Damn!

Paul gave an embarrassed cough.

"Vanessa Cartwright. You've got my card."

"Ah, yeah. Sorry… *Vanessa.* I didn't get much sleep last night."

"Late one, I bet?"

"You could say that."

He'd burned the candle at both ends, working late, clearing up after the late-night revellers had polished off the final remnants of the wedding food. And then, taking Dan, his son, to get the first train out of Holyguard that morning.

Dan was off to start his basic training with the Royal Marines on Monday. Thirty-two weeks of unadulterated hell.

What he'd give to go back to that again. To be nineteen again, like Dan.

Paul pointed to the large canvas structure and the side frame.

"So, all this is coming down today?"

Vanessa flicked her eyes over her phone.

"Yip. Team's arriving early afternoon to pack it up ready for the wedding next weekend. But, we've gotta get these trestle tables out of the way first."

"Wow. Looks like quite an operation."

"Yeah, we've got four marquees up this weekend. We usually move them Monday, but there's a gale blowing in later."

"And you do this all on your own?"

She cocked her head making her long ponytail swing.

"Is that a subtle way of asking me if I have a husband, Paul?"

His eyes widened. She was nothing, if not direct.

"No. Uh… I meant that it looks like a lot of work, that's all."

"For a woman?"

Argh! He was digging a massive hole for himself. He rubbed his hand across his shaved cheek, wrong-footed and unsure of what to say next.

Vanessa shrugged it off.

"It's okay. I get it a lot. It is heavy work, but with marquees, logistics is the biggie. Getting everything to the right place at the right time. Especially when the wedding season's at full pelt. But, hey! It's fantastic to be a part of people's special day. And when the tents are all dressed up with lights and the tables are decorated, they look magical."

She moved to his side and showed him her Instagram account.

Paul was impressed. And not just with the marquees.

"Big Top Tents...Why *Big Top*?"

"*Ahh*, well. I'm from a circus family. It all finished when I was a kid, but I guess working with tents, putting them up then packing them away, it must still be in my blood."

"And no lions and clowns still hangin' round?"

He caught her eye and she smirked.

"Are you asking me if I have a boyfriend, Paul?"

He was caught out again. What was this woman like? But she was right. He kind of had been.

She held his gaze.

"No boyfriend."

"So, if you ever did want to go out sometime?" he chanced, unable to help himself.

"You've got my number on the card I gave you last night."

Her phone went off.

"The guys are here. Nice meeting you, Paul."

She flashed him another broad smile, then picked up the call and walked away. Two of her workers began collapsing the trestles and carrying them over to a trailer behind a large SUV.

Paul watched her working. He didn't do dating. What had possessed him to stick his neck out, like that? He wasn't a spur of the moment kind of guy. But Vanessa Cartwright was different. He wanted to know more about her. Maybe, it was her self-assurance? Or her circus family background? More likely, it was that cute butt of hers that he was still studying as she helped move the trestle tables.

His sons kept telling him that it was time he got out there again. Things still hadn't resolved themselves, though. He was still suffering.

He found her card in his coat pocket. He'd deal with all that other stuff later down the line. She had to agree to go out with him first.

13

◆ ◆ ◆

Alys let herself into Leo's luxury apartment in the exclusive sixth arrondissement.

"Leo? Mon coeur, c'est moi. Leo? I'm back," she called in her faltering French.

She'd been in Paris two years, working at La Patisserie Celine, where she was honing her dessert-making skills under the tutelage of world-famous pastry chef, Celine Martin.

Leo's luxury apartment was quite a step up from the cramped box room digs she'd been renting before.

It had certainly been a whirlwind. In the space of two months, she'd fallen passionately in lust and then in love with Leo, a French financier and the man of her dreams. Alys called it her 'Summer of Love.' And where better to be, than the city of romance?

They'd bumped into each other in a bar. By that night she was in his bed, and the following weekend she'd moved into his apartment. Crazy, crazy love. And she'd been gloriously swept away by it.

He'd showered her with gifts. Taken her to triple-starred Michelin restaurants and hip brasseries that only the Parisians knew about. He'd even flown her off to Antibes where he surprised her with a table at the exclusive Mirabelle's.

They'd eaten langoustines in lemon thyme, paired with a chilled 2016 Chateau de Sharon Pouilly Fume wine. And, they'd made love all night in their private villa to the sound of the waves slapping against the rocks of the Cap D'Antibes. It had been like a dream.

She had what she imagined every woman wanted. A sophisticated, handsome, fabulously wealthy boyfriend. And a perfect life.

So, why then, when Owen Morgan placed his lips onto hers at the wedding, did it leave her in such a hot mess? And why had the memories of his hot built body been in her head all the way back to Paris?

Putting her bags down on the polished parquet floor, she wandered through the empty apartment.

It was Monday afternoon, but there was no sign that Leo had been there at all through the weekend. The dishwasher she'd put on before she'd left was still stacked with dishes. Now clean.

She opened the large wooden blinds on the full-length windows in the lounge. There was no sign of his distinctive black Porsche in the street below.

Feeling a little lost in the huge, empty apartment, she drifted back to the bedroom to shower and change.

Later that evening, a portion of stuffed chicken breast and vegetables still sat untouched on a plate ready to be microwaved when Leo got in. Alys had eaten hers long ago and it was now getting late, considering both of them worked early mornings.

Her phone went off.

She grabbed it from the charging point. Leo?

It was a message from Owen. Rhys must have given him her number.

She opened it.

'Hope you got back safely. See you in a couple of weeks.
Owen'

What was his game? And why had that little text made her pulse race so fast?

She typed back.

'Owen Morgan, I know you've got a thing for my puddings,
but you are such a tart! You've got a girlfriend, so please
don't text me again. Alys

BTW - I'm in Paris, not Wales, so the chances of me seeing you in a couple of weeks are pretty slim'

A few seconds later her phone pinged again. He wasn't giving up.

'No girlfriend. As I said, I'll see you soon. Owen x

BTW- Ever think of taking up boxing? You've one hell of a right hook.'

She cringed. Her fingers hovered, poised to type an apology. In the end, she resisted. The slap served him right.

Owen laughed out loud as he read her text.

A tart, she called him. He'd rather label himself as a strategic opportunist. A worshipper of beauty. And Alys certainly needed someone to worship her.

She'd been on his mind for about six months now. Since the day he first saw her, covering for Beth in La Galloise restaurant in Freshwater Bay.

With her long auburn hair and her delicate face, he'd not been able to take his eyes off her at Rhys' wedding. Those Jessica Rabbit curves of hers, coupled with the most spectacular breasts he'd ever seen on any woman. There was no denying it, Alys Edwards had been blessed.

Yes, she was worth the chase. He'd even signed a year of his life away with a top French rugby team, so he could do just that.

He lingered on the picture he had of her in his head. And remembered that dessert she'd made. Smooth, dark chocolate mousse with a honeycomb crunch. It was the best damn thing he'd ever tasted. Still was.

He chuckled to himself. How could he ever resist her puddings?

It was the first light moment he'd had in what could only be described as a gruelling weekend.

In hindsight, allowing Julia to browbeat him into taking her to the wedding had been a big error. It had certainly stuffed up his chances with Alys, and had made for some awkward questions later from his parents.

Julia had fought with him all through Sunday. She'd woken up pissy, still whining on from the night before about commitment. And she was nothing short of rude to his folks through the roast dinner his mam had made them. It had been written all over his mother's face. She didn't like Julia one little bit. And he didn't blame her for that.

By the afternoon, he'd done the walk on the beach and the 'we-need-time-apart-to-find-out-what-we-want-in-our-lives' speech.

They'd driven back to Cardiff in sullen silence. And then she'd turfed him out of his bed. She commandeered that and forced him to spend an uncomfortable night in the spare room. He was glad about that, though. Sex would only have complicated the message. And all day, he'd been crystal clear with her. They were done.

This morning, she'd slunk out of the flat early, catching the first train out to London. And he'd not heard from her since. It was for the best. Julia was angry with him. But he had a hunch that it was her plans, rather than her heart, that he'd upset.

If he flicked on the TV she'd be on there, right now. Sat on the presenter's sofa, broadcasting live to the masses. A fake smile plastered across her face, bantering with some comedian about his new autobiography.

He folded up the signed solicitor's papers and slid them carefully inside the envelope to post. He was off to Paris at the end of the week.

The average career of a professional rugby player was seven years and he'd done ten, which he'd managed to combine with university study. He'd been lucky so far, with only a few back injuries and a cauliflower ear. And with million-pound contracts in club rugby these days, this last signing was his retirement fund.

Good job too, because he'd blown a chunk of his nest egg buying two things he never thought he would; his brother Gareth's boathouse and The Lobster Pot Inn.

Gareth had mentioned that the owner of The Lobster Pot had put the place on the market; and that although Beth had a signed lease, it made things uncertain for her business. She'd taken the place over while her restaurant was being rebuilt, but longer term she saw the inn and La Galloise working hand-in-hand.

On paper, the inn was a sound investment, mainly because Beth was running it. And within a few minutes, Beth had convinced him that he'd be a fool not to invest. Property values were on the rise. Whichever way he looked at it, she was right.

He'd insisted on the deal remaining confidential. Just Gareth, Beth and himself. No more in the family to find out yet. He didn't want it spread about that he was a flash git.

The boathouse was more of an impulse buy. He'd never thought that he'd move back to Freshwater Bay. His life had always been in Cardiff. But when Gareth explained how the boathouse was too small for his growing family, he'd started considering it more seriously.

It was one cool house. The lime-white wooden floors and Scandi-modern interior. The huge bi-fold windows and the sea all around. If nothing else, it'd make a great holiday home. And when he thought about it some more, he couldn't picture another place he'd rather be.

Gareth and Beth were delighted. It would bankroll their new family home.

CHAPTER 3

----------✳----------

S he'd told Leo that she wouldn't be back until six, but then Celine had juggled the shifts around so she wouldn't be doing twelve hours straight on a Saturday. The bakery was hard work with insanely early starts, but she didn't mind. She'd learned so much since she'd been working there.

Walking through the Paris streets mid-afternoon, Alys felt like she'd gained a whole day. Nope. It didn't get any better than this. The warm sun. Everyone looking happy. Relaxing, socialising in one of the most sophisticated cities in the world.

Her early finish would be a nice surprise for Leo too. He'd been complaining about her weekend shifts. It was a big inconvenience, he'd told her. He liked to get out of Paris on Friday nights. Hang out with his friends. Destress after a busy week on the financial markets.

He usually insisted they eat out on the weekends. If she pleaded, she wondered if he'd agree to stay in tonight? Just the two of them. Let her spoil him, cook him a delicious meal.

He'd been coming home late all week, complaining that he was too tired. Tonight they could have an early night. Spend some quality time together under the covers. Try to get things a little spicy between them again.

"Quatre-vingts euros, s'il vous plait."

Jeepers! They were a very nice bunch and all. But eighty euros for petals and leaves? Ten days and they'd be in the bin.

Owen sighed and exchanged his hard-earned cash for the big orange spray. Paris was expensive.

The rugby club had found him an apartment near the training ground in a quiet residential area, not far from the Eiffel Tower. It suited him fine. It felt soulless but it was fine as a place to rest his head. And it had a spare room if any of his friends or brothers fancied a Paris mini-break.

He'd done a couple of training sessions with his new squad and he'd coped with the cardio easily enough. They were no harder than the ones he'd done in his previous club. His old back injuries were healed, his fitness was as good as it had ever been, he was in great form for the season.

Playing centre position in rugby meant taking hard tackles. He drew the big boys in to create space for faster, lighter players outside on the wings.

It was a strategic position. He was the playmaker. The man who found the space, who sidestepped and swerved his way around his opponents to set up the passes to score the try. And he was damn good at it.

But every now and again there'd be a disconcerting click, followed by a pull, a snap or a shooting pain. Not to mention the physical knocks from each match he played. His opponents were all giants, like him. Shoulders battered into and regularly dislocated shoulders. Knees cracked ribs. Heads were piled vertically down onto the ground into neck-crunching crushes. Rugby was a hard, physical game. He tried not to think about that too much. He was a tough bugger. And fortune had favoured the brave.

He hoped it would now, too. He'd got Alys' address from Gareth. Her apartment was a forty-minute walk away, located in what appeared to be a very swish part of the city, not that far from Notre Dame cathedral.

The rental price of apartments in Paris was painful. Alys was living in some style, he decided as he walked along the historic streets towards the address. This postcode was way beyond the salary of a pastry chef.

With his newly purchased bunch of flowers in one hand, he rang the outside buzzer by the side of a dark navy door.

He couldn't wait to see her reaction when she answered. She'd be shocked, but hopefully, pleased to see him and not still annoyed about that kiss. He still thought about that a lot. He'd been in no doubt that she'd wanted it too. And what a kiss it had been. Just the perfect amount of hot to make him want more.

The slap he'd had for it, that was all about Alys covering her arse. A public rebuke for kissing her when he had a woman in tow. He'd deserved it too. It'd been a bad thing to do, in front of everybody.

It hadn't gone unnoticed, either. Gareth had teased him afterwards, and his mother had given him grief. But, then she'd been delighted when he told her that he'd ditched Julia.

He'd deliberately chosen this rare Saturday afternoon he had off from playing, hoping it'd be a good time to catch her in. When he'd asked Gareth, Beth hadn't been sure what shifts Alys worked in the bakery, but she was sure that it would be early mornings.

Once the season got going, the rugby clubs played every fortnight. His away games were dotted all over France. It was a familiar routine. Playing Saturday afternoon, he was usually back by Sunday and sore. Monday and Tuesday were for resting, before the training and preparations began again ready for the next weekend's match. Perhaps she'd have Monday or Tuesday off too?

There was no answer from the intercom by the main door. He tried another button, hoping to beg his way in, even though his French was pretty hopeless. No response.

He was on the verge of giving up when the front door opened and a young mother edged out backwards from it, pushing the door with her shoulder as she manoeuvred a toddler in a pushchair onto the street. He held the door for her with his free hand

21

and then slid in after her.

Inside was a large spiralling staircase with an elaborate wrought-iron railing. There was an ancient-looking iron elevator to the side. Way above his head, a cascade of crystals dropped down from the ceiling, glistening in the sun coming in through the skylights. A full-on chandelier.

Nope. Alys was definitely not slumming it.

He climbed the stairs to the second floor. Then, taking a deep breath, he rang the apartment doorbell. His heart was thumping. He hadn't realised how alone he'd felt in Paris. If she wasn't there, he'd leave the flowers propped up against the door. Then text her.

Owen braced himself as he heard someone inside the apartment approaching. The door swung open and he held out the bunch.

"Oui?"

Owen's face dropped.

A tall, dark-haired man in his mid-thirties was standing in the doorway. Naked, save for a tiny towel tucked around his slim waist.

In the background, a woman called out in husky native French.

"Qui est là, Leo?"

Leo. Owen was confused.

No way was that Alys' voice. And he'd definitely interrupted something. The bedhead hair and the pissy frown on the guy's face told him as much.

"Sorry, I...uh... I've got the wrong apartment," he apologised hurriedly in English.

Taking a long sneering look at Owen and the flowers, without another word the man slammed the door in his face.

Back outside, Owen checked his phone. It was the right address.

Was this 'Leo' her flatmate? Or was it her lowdown, no-good, cheating boyfriend? Or, had Gareth given him dud intel? Whatever it was, something was off.

He bit the bullet and gave Alys a call.

◆ ◆ ◆

Her phone went off in her bag.

"Alys, where are you?"

It was Owen, she was sure. She recognised his deep lilting Welsh voice.

"Paris."

"*Duh*. Where?"

"I'm on my way home. I finished work early. Why?"

"What's the address?"

She rattled it off for him.

"And where are you now?"

"About ten minutes away. I'm walking through Luxembourg Gardens. Why? What's this about, Owen?"

"Wait there. I'll meet you... I'm just around the corner."

The call ended abruptly. He sounded rattled.

When she'd caught up with Beth, she'd told her that Owen had signed for a Paris club. And Alys couldn't deny that it had made her curious about whether he'd be in touch. She'd secretly been hoping he would.

And now, here he was.

She spotted him walking towards her through the park with a huge bunch of flowers in his hand. For her. And she could see the smile plastered across that handsome rugged face of his.

Her pulse raced. Oh God! She'd forgotten how hot he was.

His dirty blond hair was a little tousled. And those bright blue, almost turquoise eyes that twinkled wickedly at her when he spoke. Her hands knew what that chiselled jaw of his that had taken more than a fair few knocks on the rugby pitch felt like. She remembered the taste of his lips and that kiss...

Get a grip, girl, she warned herself. This attraction, crush even, it was wrong. She had a man. And it didn't take a rocket scientist to work out Owen Morgan's strategy.

This was a game. He was hunting her down. And she had no intentions of becoming his prey.

"Hey!"

He held out his arms to pull her into an embrace.

She stepped back.

"Oh no! I'm a mess."

Her chef's uniform was floury and she'd managed to get a big yellow stain across it.

And her hair. She'd tied it quickly into a messy bun after she'd taken off the hairnet they all had to wear. She was a plain floury shadow of that glamorous wedding guest he'd kissed.

"Alys, you always look beautiful."

He was a flatterer, alright. And he was now studying the stain across her chest.

"Is that custard?"

"Passionfruit syrup."

He eyed her quirkily.

What ideas were bouncing around in his head? The same as in hers? Passionfruit syrup smeared all over... She cleared her throat.

"Great to see you, Owen."

They kissed each other on each cheek in a typically French way, and then found a bench. It was busy in the gardens, with families and couples walking the park's long avenues. The leaves of the large plane trees had turned a rusty gold, and like the sun, the afternoon was mellow and warm.

"Nice not to have a slap when I kissed you this time."

That cheeky smirk of his would be her undoing.

"You only feel my fist if you stick your tongue down my throat."

She flashed him an angelic smile and straightened her jacket as she sat. It was surprisingly good to see him. A little piece of home in Paris.

"I called at your apartment."

"Did you meet Leo?"

She noticed how Owen's cheek twitched.

"Is he your boyfriend?"

Alys kicked at the gravel path with her trainer.

"Yeah."

"Oh... uh... There was no one in."

"Leo said he might go out."

She put the bouquet to her nose, smelling the delicious floral notes of the elaborate bouquet. A riot of oranges matching the autumn colours. She put them carefully down beside her.

"These are gorgeous. Thank you."

She paused, studying the exotic spikes of the bird of paradise.

"Owen, I'm sorry. I should've told you I had a boyfriend."

She glanced up at him. His face unreadable.

"I already knew. Beth said."

Alys raised an eyebrow. Her friend was usually uber-discreet. And she wasn't sure why Beth would even have been talking to Owen.

Owen gave her a nudge.

"No reason we can't be friends though, eh? I don't know anyone else in this city, apart from rugby dudes, and I need a tour guide to show me around."

"Sure. Why not?"

She didn't know Owen as well as Rhys and Gareth, but she'd talked to him enough to know instantly that they could be friends. A very hot friend she'd shared a sizzlingly kiss with. One who she was having forbidden passionfruit syrup fantasies about.

She shifted a little, finding her bag and checking the time on her phone. She couldn't quite control her nerves around him. He made her edgy.

"I'd better be getting back. Leo'll be home soon."

Owen stretched out his legs on the park bench.

"Chill, Alys. It's Saturday afternoon. Leo's not expecting you yet. You've been working for hours and we've got the best seats in the park. I'm sure he won't mind if you hang out here for a bit. It's so nice."

She relaxed back on the bench. She wasn't in any rush to go. It was great to see him again.

Leo hadn't been spending much time with her recently. Au-

tumn was one of his busiest times, he'd told her. And network-
ing was an important part of his work too. Wining and dining
clients after work and at weekends. If he wasn't at the apartment when Owen had called, he'd probably be gone for hours.
And that cosy meal she'd planned? It could well wind up being
another evening of eating alone. A glass of wine and Netflix for
one.

"Alys?"

Owen broke her thoughts.

"Spare me an hour, will ya? I wanna get to that glass pyramid
thing I've seen in the photos."

Alys shook her head.

"You mean over there, at The Louvre?"

He grinned.

"Yeah. Ever been?"

She hadn't, she was ashamed to admit.

Owen was blatantly playing for time. But, she didn't care. The
sun was shining and the only pressing thing she had to do was to
put that huge bunch of flowers he'd bought her into a vase before
they wilted.

"The Louvre, eh? Think they'll let me in with these?"

CHAPTER 5

---------*---------

Paul wasn't sure how you dated anymore. So, he'd suggested to Vanessa that they go for a walk along the coastal path. By the tone of her voice, the initial surprise followed by the quick agreement, his suggestion had been a good choice. It was a lot easier than going straight for a dinner date.

And now, here, sitting on the bench by the harbour wall outside The Lobster Pot, he suddenly felt butterflies in his stomach as she walked towards him from her parked truck. It was a strange feeling, like he was a teenager again.

She was wearing proper walking gear, a raincoat and leather boots. That was a good sign. He liked practical women.

He greeted her warmly with a kiss on the cheek, showed her the route on the map, and then set off with her along the footpath up onto the Pembrokeshire clifftops.

Studying the map the night before, Paul had planned a nine-and-a-half-mile circular route around the lighthouse to the next large beach where they'd pick up a footpath through the countryside leading them back to Freshwater Bay.

The scenery was dramatic. Sandstone and limestone cliffs. Layers of each rock type sandwiched and squeezed together in a geological war for domination. The limestone stubbornly jutting out into the sea in dramatic stacks and arches, the sandstone eroding away and forming tiny sandy inlets and huge sweeping bays.

Paul and Vanessa edged closer towards the sheer drops in front of them. Smooth limestone rockfaces were sprayed with plumes of white guano where sea birds nested in the spring. And above the waterline, Paul noticed a row of caves, like a machine gun burst along the wall of rock.

"You're not afraid of heights, are you?"

"No. But, this is some view. Good call, Paul. It's so long since I've done this. You live here, and you forget how stunning it is."

"Yeah, I was brought up in Birmingham. We only ever saw the sea a couple of times when we went on holiday."

"What made you come here?" she asked.

"Moved out this way after I left the army. I was working in a hotel down the coast."

"Army?"

"The Paratroop Regiment."

"A para eh? A good man to have in a crisis, then?"

"Hmm, p'raps. Thankfully, my days of crisis management are long gone."

They walked past an old whitewashed cottage, set in the side of the bank above a small sandy cove.

Rhys was sitting drinking coffee in the garden, grading a pile of papers. He called out to them as they went by.

"Ah! Big Top Tents lady. Paul. Great wedding."

He came over to the gate.

Paul ignored Rhys' quirky grin at seeing the two of them. He gestured at the piles of papers that Rhys had weighted down with the coffee mug on the table behind him.

"You look busy?"

Rhys let out a yawn.

"You wouldn't believe the marking I've been having to do. Never did any homework when I was in school. Kids these days, they're far too conscientious."

"You keep on loading Sam up. He loves your drama classes. Says you're sick, whatever that means."

Rhys glowed at that. Though he was still doing his training, by what his son had told him, Rhys was a natural-born teacher.

"Sam's a good lad. You should be very proud of him. And Dan."

Paul nodded. He was. And the split with their mother hadn't been easy for either of them to handle. She'd remarried and had a little girl with her new husband. His sons saw her a lot less these days.

Rhys went back to grading papers and they walked on. Past the lighthouse by the headland and down to a much larger bay where they stopped at a beach cafe.

Paul grabbed an outside table, and they ordered some lunch. It was pleasant. The conversation flowed easily. And there was no denying that Vanessa was a beautiful woman. She appeared to be enjoying his company, too.

"No gangs packing up marquees today, then?"

"No. We're pretty much done now until April."

"So, what'll you do over winter?"

"Yoga. Fitness. Believe it or not, I teach mindfulness. And I travel a lot. Mainly to South East Asia."

Paul had travelled the world with the army. But, they weren't to places you'd visit on holiday. It was usually as part of relief efforts after hurricanes and earthquakes. The occasional tour of duty. Iraq. Afghanistan.

He only saw those places at night now. In his head, when the terrifying dreams took hold and transported him back there.

Always to Sangin.

Holed up on all sides, fighting off the Taliban insurgents with two young squaddies, he was helping them to get out of there. Covering for them. Crouching in a corner behind a concrete wall, his gun was levelled vigilantly as the boys made a break for it and ran towards the chinook. They were no older than Dan.

And the policeman who was working with them as the fixer was waiting. Standing by the helicopter. The look he gave Paul, even from that distance away, he'd seen the whites of his eyes in that split second before the white of the blast.

The first wave flung him to the ground. Pushing the air faster than sound. Piercing down through his ears into his brain like hot needles. Leaving the world silent around him as he lay in the dust. Lifeless.

Policeman turned Taliban. Friend turned foe.

The bits of the boys and the suicide bomber were strewn across the field. All mixed up together. There was no sentimentality in a bomb blast. The flag-draped coffins were screwed down tight.

If only he'd have looked at the fixer's hands, not those eyes. He could have stopped it. Saved those boys.

Guilt. Depression. And the nightmares. They'd cost Paul his first marriage. And he'd shied away from relationships ever since.

He wasn't sure if he could do this with Vanessa. But, something about her made him determined to have another shot at it. She was intelligent and sharp, and he enjoyed her company. It didn't have to be anything more than that, yet.

When they got back to the harbour, he asked her if she'd like to do it again, and she agreed. Next time, they decided, they'd try something more challenging. Climb a mountain. Take the whole day.

Alys sat next to Leo at the table with his friends. It was Saturday evening and they were all hanging out at an artsy bistro not far from the river.

It had started well enough and everyone was polite with Alys, Leo's new British girlfriend. But after a while, they'd forgotten about her and they'd drifted into fast colloquial Parisian French.

Alys was quickly lost and she'd spent most of the evening silently at his side whilst Leo engaged in a passionate argument about French politics. He'd turned her world upside down when they first met. He'd made her feel so special. But here, tonight, he'd left her isolated, looking stupid.

And lately, he'd been off with her. Moody. Like she was one big regret, a bit of bad luck that he couldn't shake off. A piece of gum on his designer shoe.

Was that fair? She wasn't sure. It was only a vibe, and it could be all her doing. Hormones? Her insecurities, that haunted her like demons? Still, she wished she could follow more of what was being said. Her French was passable, but she couldn't keep up with this.

She took a sip of her red wine and smiled pleasantly at Sofia who sat opposite her, trying to start a conversation.

Sofia regarded her coolly, deigning to curl her mouth in acknowledgement, then joined in the conversation with Leo. Sofia didn't find her worthy of any attention.

Her real friends Beth and Jo would soon have put her in her place. And she'd like to see Miss Snooty try to keep up in a strange language, too. Not English, that was too easy. No, a language that she hadn't been taught as a kid. Like listening to her speaking Welsh with Owen?

Her phone rang, providing Alys with a welcome distraction. Getting up, she made an excuse to find a quiet corner to take the call.

"How's it going?"

Weird. She'd been daydreaming about him, and he'd called her.

"You're in Paris?"

"Home game. Where are you?"

"Out with a bunch of Leo's buddies. In a bar in Grenelle."

She paused. There was silence down the line.

"Is everything alright?"

"Yeah sure," she started. Then stopped. No, everything wasn't all alright. She was two steps from tears.

"Want me to come over?"

He'd picked up on her mood.

"Oh no, it's fine."

"Say the word, Alys, and I'll be there."

It was tempting. It would annoy Leo, but she didn't care. He'd abandoned her all evening.

"Come over," she found herself uttering. "I'll keep an eye out for you."

And when she spotted Owen filling the door frame half an hour later her spirits lifted more than they should have.

Without anyone noticing, she slipped from the table to greet him. He towered over the other customers; a giant. Her eyes roamed over his huge shoulders and expansive chest as he ordered.

"Thanks for rescuing me," she said a little breathily as he handed her a drink and they found a couple of stools to sit on near the bar.

"No problem. I'm glad to get out of the apartment."

"Paris not quite living up to expectations?"

He shrugged and took a swig of his beer.

"Put it this way, it's not like playing rugby with the boys back home. It's only for a year. But, I dunno, there's not the same camaraderie. And then there's the language barrier."

Alys regarded him flatly.

"I'm not feeling sorry for you, Owen. How much is this year worth to you, again?"

He raised an eyebrow at the mention of his million pound contract.

"It's a tough game. I put my body on the line every weekend."

Her lips twitched.

"Yeah, right."

"You're looking stunning tonight, Alys."

How could he do that? Make her heart pound with a throw-away line, like that?

She was wearing tight jeans and a low cut black blouse that gave a hint and a half of her cleavage. Her long auburn hair flowed loosely over her shoulders. She'd made an effort.

His eyes were still assessing her, filling her with heat. This wasn't usual. It never happened with Leo.

She put it down to her crushing on him. He was a rugby super-star, after all. And now he was her friend.

She shook off his flirtatious attentions.

"Come meet everyone."

She moved off the stool and gestured towards a table.

"Towel Guy."

"What?"

"Ahh... nothing."

But, Leo had seen them, and he was now staring at Owen. If she didn't know any better, she'd swear he was shocked. But then, Owen was a big man. When he walked into a room, people noticed him.

"Let me introduce you."

She took his hand and they sat down together. Everyone squashed up to make room for Owen's considerable shoulders.

"This is a friend of mine from home. Owen plays professional rugby."

Leo's smile didn't reach his eyes.

"Pleasure to meet you."

The group talked rugby for a little while before diverting back to their favourite topic of politics, losing Alys and Owen, who drifted into their own conversation.

Later, leaving the bistro Alys and Owen lagged behind Leo's friends, who were saying goodbyes and trying to catch the attention of taxis driving past.

"Thanks for coming out. I'd better go."

Leo had crossed the road and was having a heated discussion with a taxi driver.

Owen bent his head down towards hers.

"Still up for that city tour?"

"I'm not sure what Leo will... "

"Ah come on, Alys. What else'll you be doing all day? Ironing his shirts?"

It was depressingly accurate.

"See you Monday, then," he whispered in her ear, stealing a kiss on her lips before moving sharply away.

Alys' eyes followed him, then sought out Leo.

He was staring at her by the waiting taxi. She was sure he'd seen the kiss.

As the apartment door closed behind them, he rounded on her.

"*Christ,* Alys. You should speak English or French when you're out with us, you know?"

"Welsh's our first language. And we'd got lost with the French."

"*Pfft!*"

She'd had a taste of his temper, his passion before. But, this was different. His tone was sneering. Cold.

"Your *friend*? Is he here for long?"

"Until June."

Alys noticed the sarcastic accenting of friend. He was suspicious. Jealous, perhaps?

Whatever was going on in his head, it wasn't up for further discussion. He slammed the bedroom behind him, leaving her alone in the lounge.

She sighed.

Leo didn't like Owen.

Well, she wasn't sure how much she liked Leo much either, these days. She hated to admit it, but after their summer of love, an autumn chill had settled between them.

CHAPTER 6

---------✳---------

From their picnic spot on the grass by the side of the Sacre Coeur steps, all of Paris stretched out below them.

Alys sat down on the blanket she'd laid out.

"This is the view."

"Doesn't get any better than this," Owen agreed, ogling her cleavage as he bent to sit down beside her.

He lay back flat and closed his eyes.

She opened up her backpack.

"And you'd not heard of Sacre Coeur before today?"

His mouth curved.

"Eiffel Tower and the Arc De Triomphe. That's about it. Oh and that pyramid thing. Everyone knows that's the Louvre."

Her eyes narrowed and she jabbed his stomach with the baguette she'd bought. Always the player.

They'd done a marathon tour from the Plas de Concorde, past the Moulin Rouge, up to here. Sacre Coeur always reminded her of the Taj Mahal or a Turkish mosque, with its white spiky domes pointing to the heavens like minarets.

He propped himself up on his elbows.

"You tired?"

"Nah, it's been good for my fitness. I should do more of this on my days off. I've forgotten to be a tourist. I need to explore the streets again."

She hadn't been an expert guide by any means, but they'd had fun getting lost together. And Owen was great company.

What was going on behind those eyes, she still couldn't tell. Although, there was no doubt that he had a deep appreciation of her curves. But, then it was Owen Morgan. He was a serial womaniser. What did she expect?

Alys laid out the picnic onto paper plates. She'd brought pâté, soft cheeses and fresh baguette. She popped open a jar of home-made chutney and produced some black grapes. As a treat, she'd brought two of her homemade chocolate muffins.

"It's Monday afternoon!"

She pulled a face as Owen produced a cardboard box of red wine and two plastic glasses out of his backpack.

"You've carried that around all morning?"

He shrugged.

"Core strength training. Plus... four bottles in one box for a tenner. I love France."

"Tight-arsed wino."

He poured her a full glass of red and laughed as she pretended to wince when she tried it.

"Leo would turn his nose up at it, but actually, it tastes surprisingly good."

"Ah! What's he know about wine, anyway?"

"His family owns a vineyard."

She watched his face drop. He turned his attention to a group of female students taking selfies.

One caught his eye and she brazenly bowled up to them. Holding out her phone, she asked Owen to take a photo of her friends.

Treating the student to one of his cheesiest smiles, he gladly obliged. After their first round of photos, Alys watched him starting to ham it up. Getting in the middle of them, he was pulling faces, messing around with one of the souvenir berets they'd bought. Stealing the starring role in their selfies. He couldn't help himself. And neither could they.

He was such a flirt. She buttered slices of baguette as Owen talked to one of the girls. Tall, blonde, she was getting a small notebook out her bag, tearing off a piece of paper she'd written on. She handed it to him and he tipped her a small salute as she skipped away to join her gang of friends.

Strolling back towards the blanket, he slipped the piece of paper into his shirt pocket.

"You big tart. Did she give you her number?"

He grinned as he sat down, helping himself to the buttered hunk of baguette and a slice of the pâté.

"You're jealous."

She flicked her hair dismissively.

"Puh-lease. Spare me."

"So why were you staring at her like she was behind bars at the zoo, then?"

He was enjoying this.

"I so wasn't."

"You so were."

Suddenly, she sprang him. Making a beeline for his pocket, she snatched the scrap of paper.

He fought her, trying to catch hold of her wrists to win it back.

"Fanny Bernard. Plus phone number," she giggled, as he tickled her trying to get her to release it.

Rolling together on the rug, he pinned her to the ground, narrowly missing their plates and wine, covering her with his huge body.

Finally, she loosened her fist as she lay pinned flat by him on the blanket. Her breath hitched as she gazed up at him. There was no mistaking the desire burning in his eyes.

"Alys, forget that French prat. You only have to say the word and I'm yours."

She squirmed beneath him. Her heart pounding, her mind thinking a hundred kinds of wrong.

The chase she repeated in her head like a mantra. For him, this is about the chase.

"I can't. Leo's my boyfriend."

He released her instantly. Sitting back straight, he stowed the ripped phone number back in his shirt pocket.

She brushed her hair out of her face, putting her game face back on.

"Fanny Bernard. She's a university student. Twenty-two," he said quietly.

"Unbelievable. You've been here for two weeks and you're already getting Fanny."

He snickered, sending them both off into fits of laughter again.

"Christ, Owen, d'ya not get enough fresh Welsh meat in that red rugby shirt of yours?"

"You are jealous," he teased, taking a long drink of wine. "I told ya. Just say the word, babe."

"You wish."

She leaned back and shook her hair, hoping there were no bits of grass in it.

"Anyways, how could I be jealous, when I have my own sexy French boyfriend."

He finished eating his slice of baguette.

"With a vineyard," she added, rubbing it in.

"Alys?"

His eyes barrelled into hers.

He paused. Then, as if he'd been warring over whether to try them, he helped himself to one of the chocolate muffins.

"These!"

She grinned as he bit into it.

"They're so good. *Ah!*"

"You like the ganache centre?"

"Oh yeah... But, they're seriously bad for my diet. You're the chef, I need protein and low fat."

"Sorry. Eat more of them and you'll end up looking like me."

His eyes poured over her.

"Nothing wrong from where I'm sitting, honey."

Blushing, she looked away and helped herself to a grape.

"What? Can't you see the wobbly arse and the chub rub thighs?"

His turquoise eyes bore down on her.

"Why do you do that?"

"What?"

"Put yourself down? You're gorgeous."

She studied the grape.

"'Cos I hate myself. I've always been too fat."

"But you're not fat. You're curvy."

She glanced up at him and caught his wolfish stare.

"Believe me. Us men, we love curvy."

"Hmmm. Curvy, like that willowy blonde whose number's sat in your shirt pocket?"

He shifted a little uncomfortably.

"Those curves of yours are epic, believe me. But, if you do wanna get fit, I know a personal trainer."

"You do? Who?"

Helping himself to the bunch of grapes, he tore off a few and popped them one by one into his mouth.

"Me... But it'll cost you."

She gave him a withering look.

"How much?"

"Not money. Cooking lessons."

"What?"

"I'm ashamed to say it. I can't cook. You've met my mother. Can you imagine any of us boys getting a look in? She won't have us anywhere near the kitchen."

Alys smirked. Owen's mother. Once met, never forgotten.

"I open cartons. I reheat. I've even been known to put a jar of sauce on meat and onions. But, I wanna learn how to cook from scratch. To impress a girlfriend. Cook healthy food. Can you help me?"

She considered it. What harm could there be, two friends helping each other out?

"Purely as friends?"

"If that's what you want, Alys?"

"Yes. It is."

"It's a deal, then. I get you fit. You get me cooking."

CHAPTER 7

---------*---------

"**C**ome on Alys, keep running."

"I can't. I've not gone this far before."

"Come on, we're nearly there."

"Unlike you, Mr Fitness God, the only runs this lardy arse has ever had before was on holiday to India."

"Alys, shut up about your butt, will ya, and get jogging."

"Hear about my last personal trainer?" she shouted after him, out of breath. "Poisoned... Killer never found."

"Did you fill my water bottle?" he shouted back.

He grabbed at his neck dramatically, buckling at the knees, then jogging off.

As soon as she caught up with him, he sped off away from her again as a punishment.

She glared meanly as she jogged after him.

"Ha. Bloody. Ha. Who knew wheezing through Paris would be so much fun."

"It's not that far to the Eiffel Tower."

"How *not that far*?"

"Just 'round the corner."

"You said that three freaking corners ago."

"Ahh, stop your bitching and get that speed up a bit," Owen goaded her, pulling away again. "What was that you said?... You're too far behind me... I can't hear ya."

They'd got a little routine going. Mondays started with two hours of Alys swearing, cursing and moaning while he pushed her to run with him. The verbal abuse ended with a coffee. And after that, they'd shop in the local market. They'd make and eat lunch together, and then she'd teach him how to make another dish, usually classic French, whilst he recorded what she did on his phone.

They'd become his favourite times, he realised, as he watched her washing out two chicken quarters under the tap.

"So, you got that wine you like so much?"

"The classy 'ten euros a box' one?"

"Yep. Casserole these boys in it."

She placed the chicken pieces in an oven dish.

"A bunch of herbs, an onion, carrot, some stock, and she'll be putting it all out for ya tonight, pal."

He'd told Alys he was cooking for a new girlfriend. Another test.

Owen pressed play on his phone to video what she was doing.

"What's this dish called?"

"Coq au vin."

He stopped recording and eyed her levelly, barrelling her into a fit of laughter that he caught too.

"Coq au vin?"

He rubbed his hand through his dark blond hair.

"Honest to God. It's a classic. Google it. It'll be perfect for your dinner with Fanny."

"Greta."

She shook her head.

"Owen Morgan; another day, another woman."

"I'm a guy. I have needs."

What else could he say? She might end up marrying that French dork. God help her.

He regarded her quirkily as she rolled her eyes at him.

"You telling me that you don't, Alys?"

She busied herself with seasoning the chicken pieces.

"Greta's a receptionist at The Holiday Inn... She's Swedish."

"Oh well. That explains it."

She passed him a board and a sharp knife.

"Chop that onion and carrot up would ya? And watch your fingers, I'm not patching you up, like the last time."

He did as he was told, as Alys looked on. He'd been practising his knife skills and his technique was meeting with her approval.

"So what happened to Julia?"

She was fishing. The devil inside him wanted to push her. Make her squirm.

"All over the day after the wedding. Julia and me, it was only ever an arrangement."

"What? A fuckbuddy?"

He could tell she was surprised.

"Yeah. Why not? I like sex. It's a big part of who I am. How about you, Alys?"

She bristled.

"I'm not discussing that with you."

She left him and went over to the sink, filling it with hot soapy water.

"We're mates, aren't we? It's what mates do. Spill the beans. Do you or do you not like fucking?"

She concentrated on the dishes she was washing. Head bent over the sink.

"Yeah, 'course I do."

Her voice was defiant, like he'd challenged her.

And, he wasn't done yet. How far out of her comfort zone would she go?

"So, you and Leo? Is he adventurous or is he a painting by numbers kinda guy?"

She chewed her bottom lip, placing a wet dish on the drainer, considering what to say.

"It's been a bit vanilla, recently," she admitted. "But, I can get creative. I like being adventurous. Now, how are you doin' with those onions?"

He grabbed a cloth to dry up, stopping her in her tracks.

"Adventurous, like how?"

"I'm not going into this with you, Owen. It's not right."

"Come on, Alys. It's only mates talking. You'd talk like this with Beth wouldn't ya?"

"Maybe."

"*So?*... Adventurous how?"

"Owen!"

"I'm a psychologist. I spend my life delving into sexual desires."

He moved up behind her, his hands planted on the sink each side of her. Caging her against it with his body, bending his head to the side of her neck to whisper in her ear.

She shivered.

"Adventurous, like girlie's got a vibrator? Like you've bought some sexy underwear? Or is it something a bit darker? Does Alys Edwards have a kink?"

A sharp intake of her breath.

He whispered against her neck, his mouth millimetres from tasting her again, "If you were with me, I'd show you adventurous."

Suddenly, she broke free. Shoving his arm away, she pushed him out of her space and slipped away from the sink.

"Forget it, slut man."

She anchored herself back by the stove. Turning to face him, her chin raised, wooden spoon waving defensively in her hand.

"You wanna know my kink?"

"Yeah. I do."

"My kink is, I don't do casual."

"Ha!" he shrugged, backing right off. "Well, at least you're honest. Most chicks? They're all cool, at first. Then, I dunno, a switch flicks and suddenly they're wanting commitment, exclusivity, the whole shebang."

She shook her head.

"You're unreal."

"Don't look at me like that. It's God's honest truth."

Alys began scouring the cupboards for garlic.

"I dunno," she said dismissively, opening the fridge door and finding a bulb. "P'raps they think they can convert you from the man-whore you are?"

"Thinking they're the one, right?"

She let out a sarcastic huff as she slammed the garlic onto the worktop and ripped off a couple of cloves.

"Ah come on, Alys. You and me both know sex is a natural act. A bodily function. Why does it always have to get wrapped up in emotions?"

"You tell me. You're the Doctor of Psychology. But I'm *so* looking forward to seeing you when love slams into you hard."

"Aint gonna happen."

She peeled the garlic cloves and squeezed them in the press until the garlic came out in a juicy pulp.

"Bet it will. You'll be like this garlic. All mush. The time will come, Owen Morgan when you'll be so lovesick you can't breathe," she jabbed at him with the garlic press. "And you'll be counting down the seconds 'til you see your lucky lady again."

He threw her a dubious look as she pinned him to the ropes. Her eyes narrowed and her lips pursed as she carried on with another set of teasing blows.

"Of course, there'll be the snivelling, when you worry she's gonna break up with ya. The endless missed calls about some stupid misunderstanding. You'll be on your knees, a pitiful wreck, begging for another chance. And when the time comes, you'll be pledging your love in some grand romantic fashion, desperately hoping she won't break your heart."

He let out a loud scoffing laugh.

"Yeah, right."

"When you fall, which you will, it's gonna be messy."

He poured the onions into the sizzling oil and started chopping the carrots. She moved his arm out of the way and snuck in by the side of him to give the onions a stir, adding in the garlic she'd crushed.

"If that's what love's like for chicks, forget it. See this. This is cool. What we have. Hanging out. Messin' about as mates. I think this is the best way, don't you?"

"Like keeping it in separate boxes?" she ventured. "The friends box, as opposed to the fuckbuddy box?"

"Is that what you think this is?" he responded. The chemistry between them was undeniable. She was the one deluding herself.

She screwed her nose.

"I think... thank God I've chosen the right box."

"Paul, if we do go up Snowdon, would you like to stay over afterwards? I'm not suggesting anything else, don't get me wrong. Separate rooms an' all. But it'd be fun to go out. Have a meal. A few drinks. What d'ya say?"

Vanessa was broaching it carefully, but she'd reached a point where she needed to find out exactly what was going on between her and Paul.

They'd been seeing each other for over a month. In which time, they'd been walking and kayaking. They'd even done a day coasteering.

And now, he'd suggested that for their next date they have a go at climbing Wales' highest mountain. She was starting to wonder whether she was more Sherpa than girlfriend. Not that she wasn't enjoying it. But she wanted to see him in other situations. Not just look at the back of him as he led her along mountain ledges.

"Sam's at home. I'm a bit nervous about leaving him. I'll need to check with him."

She took a bite of her cheese sandwich, sitting beside him on the ledge of the open boot of Paul's saloon car.

Sam was seventeen. She was sure that he could stay with a friend or have one stay over if he didn't want to be alone? He spent most of his evenings by himself in the house when Paul was working.

"Forget about it. It was only an idea."

She scuffed at the gravel with her hiking boot and leant backwards, rolling her shoulders. Was there something wrong with her? Did men pick up the signals?

She never met anyone straightforward. And with Paul, outwardly everything was fine. But, there was an air about him too. He was guarded, like something was holding him back from any intimacy between them.

"I'm off to Laos in January. Ever been?"

Paul shook his head.

"You'd love it there. They've got these sheer karst rocks shooting out from the jungle. The climbing's amazing. And the rivers and forests... There's the Mekong, of course, but there's so much more too. It's a wonderful country, Paul. But it breaks my heart when I see how they're still struggling from the Vietnam War. Shells are still blowing their kids up. Even today."

Paul shuddered at that. He was ex-military. She needed to be more sensitive.

"What are you doing out there?"

"Travelling around, mostly. Taking some yoga classes. Mainly, getting my mind cleared. I first did it a while back. Headed off one time after things got a little... complicated, here. Now, I'm so busy with weddings that I don't have a chance to catch my tail. I need a little time off in the winter to centre myself. And in Laos, I can kick back and relax. And they have wifi, even out there, so I can still keep up to date with bookings and whatnot."

"I'm not sure I've ever done that," Paul muttered.

"What?"

"Relaxed. Totally switched off."

"You should try it. I can teach you some yoga, if you like? It'll help you after your busy shifts at the restaurant."

"Vanessa, let's go to Caernarfon."

"Yeah?"

"Yeah," he smiled, squeezing her hand.

CHAPTER 8

--------- ✸ ---------

"**M**erde! Alys, this is bullshit. What is it with you? Are you counting, or what?"

Leo was storming through the bedroom like a mad man, packing his weekend bag in his rush to get from there. And Alys was clearly not invited. Not that she could go anyway. She was working all day Saturday.

"I only said we never do much together these days," she responded trailing after him, trying to soften the edge of this latest outburst.

He stormed back from the bathroom, washbag in hand. His thinly veiled irritation with her no longer disguised.

"I'm off for the weekend. Yes. For sure. But you never make any effort with my friends when you tag along."

That again. She could have argued, but what was the point?

She couldn't tell him that his friends were barely civil to her. Or, that she wouldn't cross the street to talk to any of them if she saw them in London.

Or, that Leo made her feel hellishly lonely, even when he was with her. And that she didn't like him anymore. That she found herself trapped in this situation of their relationship.

The reality was that she'd moved in with him in a mad, loved-up rush. And she now bitterly regretted that decision. She was sure he did too. Even the lust was gone. They hadn't had sex in so long.

Instead, she kissed him sweetly on the lips as he came into the lounge with his bag.

"Have fun."

He slammed the door shut as he left. Leaving her to battle the Friday evening traffic out of the city.

Leo wasn't being fair. He didn't want her around his friends, but then he resented her friendship with Owen. He'd objected to her training with him, even though he'd noticed that she'd lost weight and toned up.

Owen was away in Toulouse for a rugby fixture. And when he got back he probably had his Sunday all mapped out. Exploring his innermost Swedish fantasies with Greta, his latest bedfellow.

She started cleaning. It was therapeutic. Plus, she felt she owed Leo, she paid no rent. He worked in finance. He was rich, he had a cleaner, but that wasn't the point. She always felt like she was freeloading, living there for nothing. Some cooking and cleaning, it was the least she could do.

How long she'd stay, she wasn't sure. Things were turning sour.

She began in the bedroom, stripping back the bed. She loved the feel of the sheets. Egyptian cotton. She rubbed one against her cheek. They always felt so cool and crisp against her skin.

If she did move out, she'd miss the luxury of these.

It was then that she saw it.

Jade green. No more than a scrap of lace tucked at the very bottom of the bed.

Pulling it out, she held it at arm's length with the tips of her fingers.

She'd stripped the bed the week before. This thong couldn't have been there then. And it was most definitely not hers.

Stunned, she got her phone out. Automatically, she snapped a picture and sent it to Owen.

'Help! What do I do?'

Owen typed back immediately. The thong had caught his attention.

Put it on. And then take the pic again so I can get a better idea of what it is ;)

Alys let out a sharp laugh. Typical.

Not helpful. I found it in the bed. And it isn't mine.

He clicked instantly to video chat. He was sitting on his bed alone in a very basic-looking hotel room. Being a sports star, it wasn't all glamour, then.

"Alys, what's going on?"

His face was full of concern.

Oddly, she wasn't too cut-up. She wasn't anywhere near tears. Maybe, it was the shock and she was still processing what she'd found? Who was she kidding? She knew exactly what Leo had been up to. And it was the end of their affair.

"Where's Leo?"

"At the coast with his buddies for the weekend. Never mind that, he's obviously shagging someone else."

"I saw him."

"What?"

"When I first met you. That day with the flowers, remember? I went 'round to the apartment and he came to the door in a towel. There was a woman there."

"Why didn't you tell me?"

"I tried, but I couldn't."

"Was it a guy thing? *You bastard!*" she railed at him. "You're meant to be my mate!"

"I am... I wasn't sure you'd believe me. Plus, I wasn't certain what the score was. And I didn't wanna hurt you if I had it wrong. I presumed things would sort themselves."

She calmed down a little as she thought it through. He was right. They had.

"What am I gonna do now?"

"What do you wanna do?"

"Leave."

"You sure?"

She nodded.

"Then come to mine. I've got a spare room."

She hesitated.

"I'm not sure."

Was it wise to stay with Owen? It would seriously cramp his style. And how would she cope listening to him bonking random women in the next room whilst she lay there alone - *wishing it was her?*

She buried that quickly. Conjuring up instead, the morning after when 'said random woman' padded through to the kitchen in Owen's huge T-shirt, making coffees and conversation with her, the flatmate.

Her options, however, weren't great. She didn't want to bother Celine.

"Alys, I'm not there much. And I'll be there even less from January on, when the Wales matches start. I'll phone the concierge and get him to give you a key. Pack your stuff and we'll move your things on Sunday when I get back."

"What about Greta?"

"Who?"

"Greta. The Swedish receptionist?"

"Oh, that Greta."

"What? Did she not like your coq au vin?"

He gave her one of his twinkly smirks.

"Turns out she was... uh... a veggie. Hey, Alys?"

She gazed back at him. His hair was gorgeously ruffled. His eyes shining turquoise, even over the screen.

"Leo was a prick. This is a good thing. You can do so much better than him."

"Hmm."

Owen was right. It was a relief.

She placed the thong on top of his pillow on the unmade bed, then started to pack.

In the end, Alys managed her move in a single taxi ride. The total of two years of Paris life. Owen had sorted out the concierge assistance and she was soon settled in his spare bedroom.

She blocked Leo in case he tried to contact her. She didn't think for a minute he would. He was sure to be as relieved as her. How could she have gone from such passion to this state of indifference in the space of three months?

How could she have gotten it so wrong? And what was wrong with her that she didn't seem to be able to keep a man who had been so in love with her at the start?

Sitting on the spare bed in Owen's apartment, Alys had never felt so alone as she did, then. Cheated on in the city of love.

She texted Beth.

She immediately replied on a video call.

"Come to Freshwater Bay, hun. Come for December, help us with the Christmas parties and then stay and run The Lobster Pot for me."

It was appealing. Her Paris chapter was closing, and nearly all her friends, except Owen, were in Freshwater Bay. The hotel would be an exciting new challenge.

It was time to go home.

"Okay."

Beth squealed with delight.

"I'll be there early December. As soon as I've worked my notice for Celine."

Sunday morning brought Alys a new burst of energy. And she was a little guilty that she was feeling so good so soon after her break-up. She should have been puffy-eyed from a night of endless crying. Awash in a sea of tissues. She should have been depressed and moping, watching sad movies and eating ice-cream in her pyjamas under a duvet on the couch.

Instead, she went for a run all on her own. And then, she shopped for ingredients to make Owen a meal for when he got back from Toulouse. Muscle Man needed protein, and she'd worked on a special menu for him.

He'd messaged her that morning to say his plane was due in mid-afternoon, so she set to cooking with a glass of red wine from Owen's great discovery, the vin en boîte.

By three o'clock, she'd prepared Lebanese chicken skewers with mixed beans. Plus, she'd made a baba ghanoush and hummus with a green salad, and a pudding of vanilla-bean yoghurt panna cotta with a specially formulated chocolate protein brownie that was under a hundred calories a portion.

The food sat ready for him. And she waited patiently. Sipping her wine.

She checked the time on her phone again, and her messages. Scrolled through her social media. Bored.

Owen was late.

Was the plane delayed? She wasn't about to text him. No way was she going to play the little wifey. The food was meant to be a surprise. A thank you for letting her stay, that was all.

But by six, he'd still not appeared. And by eight, the food was wrapped and stored in the fridge. The boîte was half its original weight.

And by eleven, Alys was slumped on the couch with red wine teeth, under a duvet watching a weepy romantic movie in pyjamas. Puffy-eyed, awash in a sea of tissues.

But that was nothing to the state that Owen was in. When he staggered up to his apartment a while later his mother would have described him as worse for wear. His brothers would have called him completely shit-faced.

"Owen? S'that you?"

Alys woke up from under the duvet on the sofa feeling wobbly, woozy and still buzzed. The film had finished and it was pitch black.

A light suddenly came on in the living area. The room was spinning dizzily around her as the harsh overhead light bore into her eyes, making her squint as she sat up.

Shit! She wasn't properly dressed. And Owen was there. His shirt was half hanging out of the back of his jeans. His hair was mussed up. And he was staring down at her, his eyes feasting on her tits.

His arm had been easily twisted on the plane, and he'd stopped at more than a few bars with some of his new 'mecs de rugby,' a.k.a. hard-drinking bad-ass rugby boys like himself.

And after a drunken discussion with half the bar, they'd all agreed. She had to go. He'd lost all his personal space, and he didn't like sharing.

He had to tell her tonight, they'd all told him. So, he was going to do it. Now. Strike while the iron's hot.

He switched on the lights as he came in.

She was on the sofa, under a duvet. Asleep.

"Alys. I need to tell yer something."

She sat up and stared up at him, like she was waking up. Unfocussed.

"I need to tell ya something. I need to tell ya … that you have to…"

He plonked himself down beside her, throwing back the duvet to get her full attention.

"That you have…"

Fuck me!

She was in short pyjamas. Squashed into a T-shirt that was far too tight.

And those boobs of hers. They were nothing short of amazing. Ripe. Perfection. He wanted to bury his face in the middle of them. Suck and tease them until she screamed out for him.

A wave of what he thought of as mushy shit swept through him, leaving him feeling tingly inside. Alys was his woman.

"I have to, what?" Alys asked.

"You have to... two spectacular... Anyone tell ya, you've got a great pair of tits."

All thoughts of asking her to leave left the tiny space in his head that he kept for rational thought. He wanted to *do* her, right there, on the sofa. She'd be up for it. She liked sex too. She'd told him.

And he was in luck. Alys stretched her arms out wide towards him, giving him an eye-full of her stupendous stacked rack through her too-tight t-shirt.

"Owen, I really fancy you."

She leaned towards him as he planted his face on hers in a big, sloppy, deep-tongued snog.

"You asked me before, what I like?"

She stretched her hands over her head. Holding them together, wrists touching.

"What? Tied? Controlled?"

She nodded.

"*Shit!*"

She broke free. Jumping up from the sofa, she bolted for the bathroom.

He swivelled around after her. Over-rotating. Falling off the couch.

"Whar's wrong?"

"I'm gonna puke."

All things considering, she was feeling quite well the next morning.

She'd showered and cleaned the bathroom. She was as fresh as could be expected, under the circumstances, and was dressed for a run.

On the way back, she popped to the small supermarket two streets away, and she was now making a fruit salad and an egg-white loaded omelette.

The shower was running.

She cringed. Owen was up and about.

It was a small mercy that he'd been even more drunk than her. And at least they hadn't ended up in bed together. That would have been embarrassing. And inevitable. Thank God she'd vomited.

When she'd got out of the bathroom, he'd been snoring on the sofa and she'd escaped to her bedroom with a pint of water and a packet of ibuprofen.

This was the last thing she'd wanted to do. Make things weird between them.

At least she'd only be in his apartment for a couple of weeks. Celine had been disappointed when she'd phoned to tell her that she was leaving. But when she explained everything, Celine had reluctantly let her go with two weeks' notice. She hated to let her down. She'd been a wonderful mentor and she counted her as a friend.

His hair still wet, Owen sloped sheepishly into the kitchen. He flicked a glance her way but didn't make eye contact.

She got on the offensive.

"How's the head, this morning?"

"Fine. How's yours?"

Yes, things were definitely weird.

"Tickety-boo, ta. Had a run this morning."

She flipped the omelette in the pan.

He stretched awkwardly around her and helped himself to black coffee.

"Fruit salad?" she asked breezily, reaching to the cupboard for a bowl.

"Yeah."

"Omelette? Extra egg whites, one yolk and some tomatoes?"

"Uh... cool."

She saw him exhale deeply, clearly relieved she wasn't going to bring up last night either.

"Did ya win?"

She sat down casually at the table opposite him with her fruit salad.

"Yeah, we scored two tries."

"Did you set them up? Tell me about the game."

And that was that. Crisis averted by food and a recount of the rugby match from Owen. Alys nodded and listened politely as every move was explained in extraordinarily thorough depth.

Nothing was said, or apparently remembered by either of them about the drunken kiss that never happened the night before.

CHAPTER 9

---------*---------

Paul checked the red digits of the alarm clock on the bedside table. It was after three a.m. and Vanessa was lying next to him in his hotel bed.

He watched her chest gently rising and falling as she breathed through her dreams. Her sleeping face was so peaceful his heart filled as he gazed down at her.

It had been so long since he'd been in bed with a woman. And he'd never been with anyone as amazing as Vanessa. She was so sorted and practical. A natural leader. He could imagine her as an aid worker, organising and helping people in crisis.

They'd had an enjoyable evening, staying over in a small tourist town after their mountain climb. They'd eaten at a little tapas restaurant near the castle walls town and then they'd strolled along the battlements to the marina.

He wasn't much of a drinker, but he'd had a few glasses of wine more than he would normally. And one thing had led to another. The upshot being that the second hotel room was lying empty. And it had been worth every penny.

He struggled to fight back sleep as he lay in the darkness, his mind drifting. He'd resolved to try and have a normal relationship, but he was still worried about staying the night with her.

In the end, he'd resolved to not sleep at all. It was the best option. He'd have to tell her about the nightmares, eventually. But that meant opening everything up. And he'd packed the incident away so tightly, speaking about it might make it worse again.

And he was functioning well at the moment. Holding down a great job. The last thing he wanted to do was to jeopardise that.

"Paul, are you alright?"

He noticed the confusion in her eyes as she started awake.

"Sorry, if I frightened you... I can't sleep."

"Then, we'll stay up together."

She pulled him to her, kissing him lightly on the lips and then disappearing with him under the sheets.

He responded eagerly. His rich umber fingers delicately feeling their way over her long body as they started making love again.

Owen was sitting on the sofa staring at his laptop as Alys wandered through from her room in his apartment.

"What are you doing?"

"A bit of reading. Psychology stuff."

Alys scanned the document on the screen. An academic paper. It looked very dry.

"I was beginning to think you'd made that whole Doctor of Psychology thing up. Thought you'd bought it from some fake African university or got it free in a cereal packet."

He flung her a look.

"Nah. I've got the certificate and the photos to prove it. Call me Owen, though. Don't worry about the formalities. None of this Doctor Morgan business. I'm very casual about the whole thing."

She gave his shoulder a shove.

"I'm doing a counselling course, if you wanna know. It keeps my brain going. When I retire from playing professionally, I'd like to be a therapist."

"You'd be good at that."

"D'ya think?"

"You helped Rhys. And you're a good listener too. Even if you do stare at my boobs when I'm speaking."

He smirked.

"I do not."

"You so do."

He shrugged.

"What do you expect? I'm a red-blooded male."

He went back to reading.

So flirting hadn't worked. What else could she do to distract him? She sat at the other end of the sofa, bored and fidgety, chewing her lip with her teeth. Shooting him looks that he was ignoring.

She hadn't told him she was leaving yet, and she only had a couple of days left. He'd been good, letting her be his flatmate. He hadn't brought any girls back while she'd been there, and she hoped she hadn't been too much of a disruption in his life. She'd tried to keep out of his way as much as she could, but it was Sunday and they were both off for a couple of days.

"I'll leave you to it," she said, getting up from the sofa. "I'm off out for a walk."

"What are you doing later?" he asked, still staring at the screen.

"Why?"

"Fancy going out?"

"Yeah, okay. A meal?"

"Cool."

"I'll book us a table at Maison Julien. I'm pretty sure it's your kinda place."

"My kinda place? Hmm... I'll be the judge of that."

She gave his cauliflower ear a flick as she moved past him.

"Trust me. You'll love it."

Owen's eyes followed her as she left. He'd been thinking for two weeks about what his rugby pals had said. He should tell her that he needed his own space, but secretly he'd really enjoyed having her around. Suddenly, Paris wasn't a lonely place anymore. And, she made him laugh. Cereal packet. Cheeky beggar.

That PhD had been eight years of hard academic labour.

He went to the fridge and ate the last piece of brownie. He couldn't believe it. Less than a hundred calories a portion, and high in protein from the oat flour and whey powder she'd used in it. Never mind that, it tasted fantastic. If she sold the recipe, she'd make a fortune.

He'd suggested they go out on the spur of the moment. He hadn't thought it through. She'd started it, by mentioning her tits. It was a flirt, if ever there was one.

Nothing had been said about that Sunday night a fortnight ago when she'd admitted that she fancied him. And her other confession, that she enjoyed playing too. So, she liked alpha men. Just as well. He fit the bill nicely. And she liked being controlled in the bedroom. No problem, either. In vino veritas.

His mind wandered to all the ways the evening might progress, and how he would finally get Alys Edwards into, or even tied to, his bed.

Getting ready to go out that evening, Alys' eyes wandered over to the hall as she glimpsed Owen in a towel coming out of the bathroom.

She hadn't meant to look up from painting her toes, but she had. And now she couldn't unsee it. He'd stood there, watching her gawp. Not moving. Letting her enjoy the view.

And what a view it was. The sight of his mighty fine, sculpted muscular body with a sprinkling of chest hair, a defined six-pack of abs and then a line trailing down from his belly button. It was enough to make a girl distracted. So much so, it made her drop a huge purple blob right across her toe.

"Shit!" she hissed, mopping up the nail varnish with a makeup pad.

Double shit! He was laughing at her.

Thank God, there were only a couple of days left. She had to tell him tonight. She was sure he'd be relieved. The prize bull could get back to his conquests. He was getting out of practice.

"Did you like what you saw?"

Owen came through to the living area, fully dressed and ready to go out. And she could tell by his twinkle that he was in the mood to tease her mercilessly.

"You wish," she blustered, still in her dressing gown and turning a hue of bright crimson.

A waft of lemon with just the right amount of woodsy musk trailed around him, sending her pulse racing.

"I swore because I blobbed. Right there. See? I blobbed my toe. That was all."

She looked down at her purple toes... *Blobbed? What the hell?*

Owen laughed out loud.

"Liar, liar, your panties are on fire. Little Miss Smart-Mouth's tongue-tied, for a change... Look at me, Alys. My face. I always feel like you're staring at my pecs when we talk."

"*Uhh*... what?"

He'd done it on purpose. He'd got her ogling at him when he came out of the shower. It was revenge for what she'd said earlier on about him staring at her tits.

"Ha!" She picked up her nail varnish bottle. "That was a very cheap shot."

"What time's this table?

She checked her phone. She was running late and he was ready to go. "Sorry. I got distracted."

She shot down his flirty look.

"*Duh*. Not you... By my toes. Gimme a sec, I won't be long."

For all her relief at ending things with Leo, she was grateful that he'd taken her to some of the best places to eat in Paris. The bistro she'd chosen that evening was her absolute favourite.

It was run by the grandson of a famous chef and nothing had been changed there since his grandfather first opened the place.

She could tell that Owen loved Maison Julien as soon as he

walked in through the door.

It was dark and authentic with old framed photographs of family members, sports teams and loyal customers by the bar. The place had stone-flagged floors, and dusty empty bottles of famous wines lined the shelving around the walls. Fisherman lamps swung from the ceiling and the tables were covered in white paper roll.

The steak was the best in Paris. Chargrilled over coals and as succulent as he'd ever tasted, he told her.

She watched him finish his steak. She was getting to know what he liked. Mostly the same kind of place as her. And the meatier, the better.

How had she ended up being friends with this Adonis of a man? The vision of his muscular chest, those sculpted pectorals with the wisp of chest hair across them, kept popping into her head. It'd been quite a distraction all evening.

"What are you thinking about?" Owen asked her, out of the blue.

"Oh, ya know. The political realities of Brexit and the implications of the technical changes to trade tariffs once we're outside the Customs Union."

Owen grinned.

"Fibber, you were daydreaming about what's under my shirt."

"What?"

Alys frowned and turned beetroot for the second time that evening.

"I've got that cereal packet degree, remember. I'm an expert on subliminal thoughts. And I recognise that dreamy look. You see my shirt and you visualise my pecs." He grinned at her. "I can pop 'em if you like."

He was getting a kick out of making her squirm. She was cursed with being so shy and girlish at times, and he could tell. It made him delight even more in trying to shock her.

"Subliminal thoughts, eh?" she retaliated, trying desperately to get back on the good foot. "Like I see your face and I want to smack it again? Or is that Pavlov?"

"It's physical attraction, Alys. You can't fight it."

"Get over yourself."

"I'm only sayin'. You see my shirt and you picture my chest. I see your blouse and I remember how fantastic your tits looked in that super-tight pyjama top. You know the one you wore that night you said you really fancied me. Right before you chundered. The night we both pretend we don't remember."

Owen stared at her as her cheeks re-reddened.

"I... I don't remember."

She looked at him steadily, her lips twitching and curling, despite her best efforts.

"Yes, you so do. We both do."

He twisted his wine glass.

"I want you, Alys. You're attracted to me too. Why don't we... ya know?"

"Owen, I'm going home on Wednesday."

His face dropped.

"What?"

"I've been meaning to tell you. After I left Leo, I handed in my notice. I'm going back to work with Beth, in Freshwater Bay. I've put on you long enough."

The cockiness had slipped away. He took a sip of his wine as he considered what she'd said.

"So, why don't we? Before you go? One night only."

Her forehead crinkled.

"Unbelievable. What am I, an itch that needs scratching?"

Honestly, it was tempting. But, she'd regret it. No, being Owen's fuckbuddy was not for her. How would they ever go back to being friends, afterwards?

"Owen, you've got a serious case of the blue balls. I'm sorry that I've cramped your style. You've been great, a true friend, and I want to keep us in that box. The friends box."

"Alys, stop talking about your box, will ya. It's distracting me"

"See, Dr Morgan? What would Freud say about that?"

"He'd say we should have sex. Straight away. There's chemistry between us. We'd be great together."

He was right. Their attraction was undeniable.

"It's not that I don't appreciate your offer."

"Appreciate your offer? What the hell? You make it sound like a real estate deal."

His face turned stony as he poured the last of the red wine into their glasses. He'd give her alpha, if that's what turned her on.

"I promise you, Alys, I won't ask again. Next time, it'll be you begging me."

CHAPTER 10

---------*---------

"Shh, hisht... It's okay.... shush... it was only a dream."
Owen was in her room.

She was sweating and her face was wet. The terror of the nightmare slammed back into her. She was back there again. Burning. Her heart was still thumping in her chest.

And Owen had seen it all.

"It's okay."

He sat by the side of her on the bed and took her to him, stroking her hair, pulling her to him. She let go as he unconsciously rubbed her back, comforting her like a child.

"Bad dream?"

She nodded, her wet face resting on his bare chest.

"I was in La Galloise, trapped in the fire. I couldn't get out. Oh God! I'm so sorry to wake you."

She spoke into his body, her breath on his skin.

"Thanks. I'll be alright now"

"Want me to stay? Purely friends. Nothing else. I'll help you get back to sleep."

"D'you mind?"

"Not at all."

He took her down with him into the bed and held her in his arms as she spooned up snuggly against him under the covers. Letting her find safety in his ample body. Helping her drift back into a deep, dreamless sleep.

When she woke up, he was gone.

She squashed the feeling of disappointment and the ache that she had when she remembered his arms around her. She was the one who'd said no. And he'd respected that, leaving her once she'd settled.

It was late, nearly ten o'clock when she wandered into the kitchen.

Owen was sitting at the table, reading online. There were two glasses of juice laid out, two empty plates and slices of melon. Over at the stove was a pan set ready, and by the side of it a jug of batter. He'd made them pancakes. He must have found the recipe online. Her cookery mentoring was complete.

"Hey."

She fidgeted with her hair as she sat down beside him.

"How are you this morning? Did you sleep okay, afterwards?"

She nodded, unsure of what to say. Thank you for holding her? That she'd changed her mind and she wanted to jump his bones?

"How often do you get these nightmares?"

He got up and poured her a coffee.

"I dunno, quite often. Every couple of weeks."

"What happens?"

For a moment she hesitated. She'd only gone into it with Rhys. Bringing it back, talking about it, made her panicky. But, Owen had seen it for himself. If anyone could help her, she instinctively knew it would be him.

"It's so real."

Her voice sounded croaky and she took a sip of her coffee.

"I can even feel the hot smoke up my nose. The suffocating smell. And the heat. It's overwhelming. Rhys is always with me. And every time we're upstairs in the flat above La Galloise. We're trapped. We both try all the doors, trying to get out, but the fire keeps coming closer. Then, the flames start licking us and the flesh on my skin begins to crackle. My hair starts to singe. That's when the roof goes. Or the floor. And we start falling, falling into the fire. About to get burned. It's like being in the pits of hell."

Her eyes fell onto his, her heart thumping in her chest. A hairline trigger between the terror of the dream and the sexual tension shooting through her every time his eyes landed on her.

He took her hand, holding it across the table.

"Alys, you've got PTSD. You need counselling."

"Can you help me?"

He nodded.

"We can try some things. Talk it through. Try some techniques to relax you at night."

She could do that.

"Sex is good too," he added, winking at her.

Heat pooled through her core. How could he play her like this? Did he have no idea how he was affecting her?

"But, seriously, talking through your dreams in detail seems to be the most powerful treatment. We can work out ways that you and Rhys can get out of that building. Visualise an escape route and talk through all the positive endings you could have in your dream. It's called imagery rehearsal treatment."

"Wow, can I try some of that cereal? I want one of those free badges too," she smiled, trying to lighten the mood and dismiss the visuals in her head at that very moment. Owen. Stripped naked. Taking her. Hard. Over the table.

She refocussed.

"And you'll help me?"

"I'd be glad to."

She took another drink of her coffee.

"Thanks for being with me last night."

"Anytime. I'm free tonight too, Alys. Remember, you've only got to ask. Or was it beg?"

Her jaw set hard. He was breaking her down. Giving her a taste. Making her want him even more. The strategist was playing her. *And dammit!* It was working.

"Bollocks!"

"What's up?" Alys called from the spare bedroom where she was packing up her things, ready for the courier. She was going back on the Eurostar.

Owen came into her room.

"Julia's in Paris and she wants to see me."

"Oh."

She hoped her tone didn't sound as flat as she felt.

"What you gonna do?"

The last thing she'd anticipated was Julia in the apartment with Owen on their last night together. His face was unreadable.

"I wanted to take you on a night walk. Grab something to eat."

That sounded good. But, judging by his eyes, still fixed on his phone, he was clearly torn.

Or was this another of his games? Trying to make her jealous. If it was, it was having the desired effect.

Alys closed the last packing box. Time for a little poker play.

"You should go. See what she wants. We went out last night."

He rubbed his hand through his hair, a little surprised.

"But, it's our last night before you go. You don't want me to stay?"

"No," she responded, as casually as she could. "I'll be fine. You should go."

She busied herself putting her summer clothes into the final box.

His phone pinged again, but his eyes lingered on her, assessing the situation.

"It won't take long. And then we'll do that walk."

"Whatever," she responded breezily. Her heart in her mouth.

By the time he left, soon after six, she was struggling to control the sickness in the pit of her stomach. One night only with Owen Morgan. Should she do it? Since when had begging become an option to consider? She dismissed it from her mind. There was no way she was going to be Owen's plaything. Hold out, she told herself firmly.

But by ten, jealousy and regret were tormenting her like demons. It didn't take a doctorate in psychology to work it out. He was in Julia's bed. He wasn't used to being rejected, and he was making her pay. Moodily, she changed into her pyjama top and shorts. Booty call for Owen Morgan.

She must have been dreaming about him. She was sure she felt his warm breath on her. The feathering touch of his lips on the nape of her neck. And his strong arms protecting her from slipping into the terrors of the fire again.

She snuggled deeper into the bed, feeling the comfort and warmth of his large body wrapped around her as she slowly surfaced from her slumbers at four a.m. to start her last day at the patisserie.

Without opening her eyes, she rolled over to the bedside table for her phone and switched off the alarm, feeling the solid, muscular arm stretched under her head and along her pillow. She'd convinced herself it was a dream.

Her eyes snapped open.

"Owen! What are you doing here?"

He was curled into her, wearing a T-shirt and jogging bottoms. Fast asleep.

She wasn't angry. In fact, it made her sad. Owen Morgan, the man whose fuckbuddy terms she could never accept, for the sake of her fragile heart.

She gazed at his sleeping face.

"Goodbye Owen."

She turned into him and kissed him lightly on the lips.

The touch was instant.

As if on a reflex, his arms caged around her. He drew her back to him, moving his mouth onto hers, under the sheets wrapped up in a passionate kiss that had now awoken everything inside Owen and her.

She felt him hard against her as his hands slipped over her breasts, her top now rolled up high. If she didn't stop it, she wouldn't be able to resist him, and she'd never make it into work.

Reluctantly she pulled away, moving herself upwards.

"Owen, I've gotta go."

"Stay," he mumbled, his mouth now sucking her nipple.

A shot of desire fired through her. He'd started teasing her nipple with his teeth. *Ach!* And nipping her. Pleasure and pain. Her thighs burned with desire. Her core thrummed. This was driving her crazy.

"Just say the words," he murmured, his fingers stretching down, inside of her pyjama shorts, feeling their way around her.

"Beg me to fuck you."

He touched her clit. *Oh God!* No way was she begging.

Unable to resist, she dipped under the covers again, finding his mouth with hers. Kissing her passionately, he demonstrated with his tongue and his fingers what he wanted to do to her.

His mouth, now on her ear, sent shivers through her. The length of him, rock hard against her. His fingers skilfully rubbing her in concentric circles, then plunging inside, finding and pressing the exact spot that could send her over the edge. And she felt herself going. There was no stopping it. She slammed hard as he worked her to a frenzy, squeezing out the last drops of her orgasm.

"Owen, please."

She could go again. She was sure. With him, this time. It'd be so good. Surely, he could see the need in her eyes.

"Say it, Alys," he mouthed in her ear. "Beg me to fuck you."

The word snapped her to her senses. This was a game. He was playing her.

"No."

He sprang away from her and sat up on the edge of the bed, still dressed.

Leaving her a panting mess, hardly able to see straight.

"Owen, where are you going?"

"Back to my bed. You've gotta get to work and I've got a plane to catch and a training camp to get to."

He was standing up now, moving across the room. He stood, watching her from the door.

"Consider your next moves carefully, Alys. If you want more, you'll have to ask me first."

And then, he put his fingers to his mouth. Tasting her. Strangely, it was the hottest thing.

"See you when you're back home at Christmas," she uttered breathily. "And Owen?"

"Yeah?"

"I won't need to ask. By then, it'll be you, begging me."

Owen got back from his training camp and opened the door to the empty apartment. He wandered through to the second bedroom. The bed was freshly made up. All her things were gone.

It was early December and he was in Paris, alone. He pulled out a can of diet soda from the fridge, popped it open and took a long swig.

Before she left, she'd made him more of those protein low-fat raspberry brownies. They were in a plastic box with a post-it label on it saying 'Eat Me.' If she asked, he would. Gladly. But, seeing the smiley face she'd drawn by the side of the instructions wiped the grin off his face.

He felt empty. Flat. And he couldn't figure out why. He really liked brownies.

Was it because she'd gone? Or, was it because he was back to square one, in a place without any network of friends? He was the psychologist, but he was struggling to suss out the basics here.

Julia hadn't helped. It had been as messy as he'd predicted. She'd a fair few gins inside her when he'd arrived. She begged him to move in with him in London. He'd told her no. It was over. He'd even told her that he'd met someone else. Not strictly true, but he wanted to test out how that felt.

She didn't believe him, of course. Owen Morgan would never commit to anyone, she'd scoffed. He'd never be pussy-whipped into a relationship. And anyway, she'd insisted, he belonged to her. That was bollocks. She'd been a good lay. That was it.

What had started out civil enough, quickly got out of hand. She was still knocking back the gins, and he'd had to get her out of the bar and take her back to her hotel. It was then that he'd made the fatal error of taking her up to her room. He'd had to scrape her off him to get out of there in one piece.

Pussy-whipped? It was nothing like that with Alys. And if he could compare the two scenarios, what he had with Julia and what he wanted with Alys, there was no comparison.

The lights were all switched off when he'd got back to the apartment. Why he'd slipped into bed with Alys, he wasn't sure. A good idea at the time, was all he'd say in his defence. He was calling her bluff for acting so casual about him and Julia. He saw the jealousy in her eyes when the text came through. She was fooling no one. It was the only reason why he'd gone. Call her and raise the bet. But, she hadn't folded. She'd held out all day, then watched him go.

But then, the whole Julia mess had taken too long and he hadn't wanted to let Alys go without feeling her close up against him again.

He didn't regret it. She felt so good as he curled himself around her. He restrained himself and simply enjoyed the feel of her. He'd never done that before. Her touch under his hands. The curve of her hip. Her soft waist as she curled up against him, finding him in her sleep. His face next to her neck. The smell of her freshly washed hair, like toffee-apples. Soft, sensuous and delicious. Just like Alys.

And then, that morning. Jees. He'd taken her. Felt her, watched her as he played her body. She was so pliable. So responsive to his touches. And when she'd come, he'd longed to take her, there and then. Plunder her, pump her hard. But he couldn't. He wanted her too much.

That was damn hot too. Her confusion and desire as he controlled her. Made them both wait. Taught them both the value of patience. He intended to take his time with Alys, not slam her like some cheap shot. Alys deserved to be sipped.

He'd given her a taste. And she hoped, like him, she craved

more. Much, much more.

CHAPTER 11

----------*----------

"I t's turkey time," Paul joked as Beth quirked an eyebrow.

They were talking Alys through the Christmas menus
and reservations. She'd only been back in Freshwater Bay a day,
but she was glad to be plunging straight into it. And they needed
her. They had wall-to-wall parties for the whole of the run-up
to Christmas, with every manner of group booked in. From local
societies to rowdy work parties, everyone was choosing The
Lobster Pot this year.

Beth sighed, and Alys understood why. The December restaurant trade was exhausting, and it didn't stretch the culinary
skills of the chefs that much. The food had to be easy to get out
and there was a lot of it. Most tables had the full three-course
meal, plus coffees and mince pies.

Still, it was great to be part of a restaurant service team again.
And there was no one better than Paul to work with when it
came to organising their busiest time of the year.

Alys mainly worked as Paul's under-chef in the kitchen, handling the junior chefs and leading on the starters and desserts.
Also covering Paul's days off.

"Any plans for tomorrow?" she asked Paul later as she read
through the jobs and ordering sheets he'd written out for her.

"Vanessa's coming over. I'm making her dinner and she's meeting Sam for the first time."

"Vanessa?"

"Yeah. We've been seeing each other since the wedding. You remember? She runs the marquee business."

Alys had a vague recollection of her.

"How's Dan?"

"He's passed his first ten weeks of basic training, twenty-two weeks of Hell to go. Dunno why he didn't become a paratrooper, like his Dad. That's kids for ya. He's here for a few days over Christmas."

New Year's Eve was their last work shift. Beth closed the business through January each year to give the staff time off to catch their breath after the Christmas rush. January was usually dead anyway, so it saved them from running at a loss. Beth and Gareth usually planned a holiday overseas, but their building projects this year had put paid to that.

Alys wasn't sure what she'd do through January yet. She hadn't thought that far ahead. But she could see that everything was in hand at The Lobster Pot. Between Beth and Paul, it ran like a Swiss watch.

She hoped that coming back to Freshwater Bay wasn't going to bore her.

He could tell that Rhys was surprised when Owen called him, wanting to talk. They were close, but it was usually Rhys who relied on his brother's advice and support.

This felt odd for Owen too. Having to admit for once that he didn't have all the answers. He'd never let emotions control him or get in the way of what he wanted to achieve. It was why he'd always succeeded at everything he did. The international athlete. He'd graduated first in class. He had everything he could hope to have.

So, why then was he feeling so flat? He hadn't been sleeping well. He was bored with everything. He moped around his apartment. Couldn't be bothered going out. He hated Paris. The new club. He was as lonely as hell. Depressed even, Dr Morgan would say.

He thought talking it through with Rhys might help. But now he was on the video chat with him, he wasn't so sure. Compared to the problems Rhys had faced, his sounded trivial. Like he was a spoiled brat.

Rhys' wife, Ariana appeared on the screen.

"Hi, Owen!"

Her face clouded over when she saw him, though she said nothing. Did he look that bad? She discreetly left Rhys alone to chat with his brother.

"What's up, mate?"

"Nothing. Why?"

"You're calling. You look like shit. What's the problem?"

Owen shook his head.

"I dunno. Bit fed up, I guess. I'm not lovin' it here. I'm counting the days, man."

Silence hung around the words as Rhys nodded but said nothing.

"I do my training. Play the matches. Go back to the apartment. It's pretty lonely. Can't wait 'til Christmas"

"Is this only about Paris?" Rhys asked. "What's *really* going on?"

Owen shrugged, but Rhys was onto it.

"I heard the Lobster Pot's got a new pastry chef working there."

"Have you seen her?" Owen asked, perking up.

"Not yet."

"Don't know what's wrong with me. Can't seem to shake it off. I was on my own in Cardiff. Had pretty much the same routine, but I was never like this."

A stupid smile was plastered across Rhys' face.

"It's not funny. Paris was a mistake. I'm showing symptoms of depression."

The bastard was still grinning at him.

"It's not depression. She's got you by the balls."

Rhys was enjoying this.

"Who has? If you're gonna take the piss..."

It was stupid to even think Rhys would understand. He was pouring his heart out and Rhys was using it to rip into him.

Rhys stared levelly at the screen. His face now serious.

"Honest, Owen. I mean it, bro. You're in love. Who is she? Was I right? Is it Alys?"

Owen rubbed his chin.

Rhys took his silence as affirmation.

"Why else are you like this? Bet, you're not talking to anyone else?"

It was true. There were no irons in the fire. He'd not flirted, chatted on social media or even looked at another woman since Alys. In spite of what she thought. Fanny. Greta. He'd been playing all of that up, trying to get a reaction from her.

"And you can't settle," Rhys continued. "You think about her constantly. You miss her when she hasn't called. Am I right?"

Owen sighed. He was.

It wasn't a huge revelation. Rhys only confirmed what Owen had been too chicken-shit scared to admit. And Rhys was right. The dissatisfaction, his loneliness, it wasn't about Paris. This was all about Alys not being in Paris with him.

She'd outplayed him. He'd fallen for Alys hard.

"What am I gonna do?"

"Christmas is around the corner. Talk to her then. Tell her how you feel. Work it out from there."

If she could only see him now. She'd tease the pants off him. Her prophesy embarrassingly was true. He was a lovesick wreck.

And he wanted her. Not as his fuckbuddy, as she called it, he wanted Alys as his girlfriend.

He was going to ask her over Christmas. If they could find a time when they weren't working, that was. When they were both in the same place.

"Hey!"

Alys' face popped up on Owen's phone, making him smile. They'd been chatting online for an hour or so most days. It kept him going. Christmas was nearly upon them.

"Busy tonight?"

"Yeah. The Lobster Pot is *party, party, party*."

"More turkey dinners, then?"

"You've no idea, pal."

"Plenty of protein, though."

"I froze down five hundred pigs in blankets yesterday. I swear, I never want to wrap another sausage in bacon ever again."

"But so worth it"

Alys reluctantly agreed.

"Hmm. Know what I'm really hating?"

Owen yawned dramatically.

"Go on. Get it off your chest."

"I'm really hating Christmas crackers."

"Ah, come on, Alys. Where's your Christmas spirit?"

"What? Pulling an empty paper roll to get a crap joke, a paper hat that falls apart and the most useless bit of tat known to man?"

"So, you're enjoying the party season, then?"

"Yeah. It's fan-flippin-tastic. I'm especially loving the Christmas songs."

Owen laughed.

"You have mentioned that once or twice."

"All day and all night. Round the ruddy real. Doin' my head in. All I want for Christmas is for Mariah Carey to shut the fuck up."

She paused and smiled sweetly at him.

"Sorry to bang on."

"That's what I'm here for. Soon, I'll be charging good money for this.

"Are you saying I need counselling?"

"Uh-huh. Christmas is causing you severe trauma. You definitely need help. We could try some of those relaxation techniques, I suggested?"

She gave him a smouldering look that made his body react in

ways she had no idea about. The intensity of their unspoken desires wasn't something they talked openly about. After all, they were still only friends. But, there was no mistaking the heat between them, even on video chat.

God, he wanted her. To taste those lips again. To lick and tease the nipples of those amazing breasts of hers. Then, take her with his mouth and make her cry out for him before he buried himself deep inside her.

"When are you back in Wales?"

"Uhh... briefly next week. Got a night with the rugby boys in Cardiff. But then, I'm straight back on the red-eye. There's a Paris game in the afternoon. I'll be back in Freshwater Bay the day after. The twenty-third. Mad eh?"

"I'm at my folks over Christmas. But, I'll see you before I go."

"Sounds good. I'm back in Paris straight after Christmas."

He was counting the days.

It sounded like they wouldn't have much time together. But, he'd invite himself to spend Christmas at her parents' place, if that's what it took. Once he told her how he felt, he wasn't letting her go.

He couldn't wait to give her his Christmas present. After he'd come to terms with his sorry emotional state, he called Ariana, a jewellery designer, and asked her to make him a pair of Celtic silver swans. She'd emailed him some pictures of her design. They were perfect. She'd set each of them on a leather lace strung through the eye of the swan so that they could be worn as a necklace.

This was a big moment for him and he was super-nervous about it all. He'd never committed himself exclusively to any woman before. But Alys was special. And he'd fallen in love with her.

CHAPTER 12

---------*---------

December was damp and dark. Alys shivered as she sat on the bench by the harbour wall in front of the Lobster Pot. The sea was still and a slate-grey, reflecting the heavy grey skies above.

She felt as flat and as cold as the air around her. There were no two ways about it, she was missing Owen.

For Alys, the realisation that she wanted Owen as more than a friend, was a leap of faith. A hope that he wasn't viewing her as a conquest, but that there was something deeper between them. She still wasn't certain. But she clung on to the tenderness that she'd felt from him when he'd held her those nights before she left.

Then, neither could she forget his hot, huge body wrapped around her. His hands on her that morning. His control over her, making her crazy for him.

He'd gotten under her skin. Got her all hot and bothered, more like. She was hooked. And she wanted all of him, now. She couldn't deny it. She'd fallen deep and she was in trouble. Unlike Leo, Owen could so very easily break her heart.

One of her first appointments back in Freshwater Bay had been to the well-woman clinic. She'd been worried about Leo's infidelities. So, she was relieved that morning when she opened the letter. She'd survived her Paris fling with no lasting souvenirs.

Getting up from the bench, she made her way to the converted chapel in the middle of the village, which was now Ariana's art gallery.

Opening the heavy oak door, she wandered inside.

She'd been struggling about what to get Owen as a Christmas present. She had a feeling he'd get something for her.

"Hey Ari, look who's come to see us, at last."

Rhys, Owen's brother, got up from his laptop behind the front desk and went over to give Alys a big hug. Ariana came out from her workshop at the back, giving a squeal of delight and another warm embrace. It was so good to see them both.

"Wow! You look fantastic. Seven months, right?"

"Yeah. Thirty-four weeks. Beth's five months along too. Must be something in the water."

"Is that right? Remind me to stick to wine and beer," Alys joked. "Are you guys on a mission to keep the primary school open?"

They laughed. There'd been talk of closing the village school, but it seemed that the population of Freshwater Bay was on the rise again.

Alys turned to Rhys.

"How's teacher training?"

"Enjoying it. I'm doing some guidance counselling too. Drugs and alcohol awareness, and supporting some of the kids."

He'd told her about his battles with addiction when he was an actor. With the support of Ariana and Owen, Rhys had turned his life around. Taking it day by day. It was certainly working. He looked great.

"Now the Christmas concert's over, I'm flat out on university assignments. Getting them out of the way before the baby arrives."

"How's Gwen?"

They were house-sitting, while Ariana's eighty-year-old grandmother, Gwen, and her boyfriend Ed were backpacking around Australia and New Zealand.

Rhys clicked onto his laptop.

"She sent Ariana into a spin, the other day."

"Why?"

"See this?"

He brought up a Facebook post. Gwen tied into a bungee harness on top of a high bridge. She'd undergone triple bypass surgery a few months before.

"From Queenstown. It was a wind-up."

"It worked." Ariana chipped in. "She's daft enough to do it."

The gallery had been super busy through November with online sales.

Alys sighed.

"I need to get Owen a present."

Rhys' eyes were smiling, though he said nothing. Ariana nudged him in the ribs.

"Stop it. Both of you. We're friends that's all. Flatmates. He let me stay at his place when I left Leo. I wanna get him a thank you present."

That did nothing to stop the two of them from grinning at her stupid.

Ignoring their smirks, Alys wandered around, scanning the shelves and the walls.

Would Owen like a picture? A seascape of Freshwater Bay? Maybe.

A ceramic pot to put on his coffee table? What thirty-year-old man wants a ceramic pot for Christmas? Dumb idea.

She was struggling. At this rate, she'd have to settle for buying him a new shirt or, God forbid, aftershave and socks.

She drifted over to Ariana's jewellery display cases. She loved her necklaces and bangles. They were so intricate.

She was agonising over whether to buy a necklace for herself when she suddenly saw it. A signet ring. On the flat top of the ring was a Celtic knot pattern. A circular knot divided into quarter segments, the spacing forming a cross.

"Ariana, what's this mean?"

She pointed out the ring and Ariana got it out of the display case.

"Ah, that's a shield knot. It's for warriors. It protects them in battle."

Alys had never thought of it before, but Owen was like a warrior in battle every weekend.

Ariana guessed the sizing. She could adjust it, she said, as she wrapped it up.

"Fancy some fresh air? I could do with stretching my legs a bit." Rhys popped the beautifully wrapped present into Alys' bag. He turned to Ariana.

"Will you be alright to man the gallery if I go for a quick walk?"

Ariana shooed them both off. She needed to finish off an order to be posted out that afternoon. To Paris. Two Celtic swans.

Rhys and Alys strolled through the village back to the harbour and began the climb up the steep hill towards La Galloise. The outer structure of the new restaurant was now in place, ready for the next phase in the new year. Gareth had got the frame, roof and the huge windows in before December. He'd been worried about the winter storms. It stood on the cliff-top, proud like a promise.

"How have things been, Alys? " Rhys asked her as they walked. "Are you still getting those nightmares?"

The fire had affected them both. Bonded them too.

"I'm trying to work through them. I was worried about sleeping in the Lobster Pot. Got a bit panicky first night. But I'm alright now. Gareth's shown me the alarm system and I'm staying in the owner's flat at the back. It's on the ground floor. I'm not sure if I'll ever get over it but Owen's given me some strategies that are helping."

"What did he suggest?"

She coloured up, but luckily Rhys didn't notice.

"Oh, the usual. Relaxation. Yoga. Stuff like that. But, he's getting me to try and go into the dream with him. I try to visualise escape routes for us when we're trapped in the flames. It's working. Last time I had the nightmare, I had a fire extinguisher in my hand, a set of stairs behind us and a window to jump through."

"Good to know you can get us both out of there."

They walked a little more in comfortable silence.

"So, what's really going on then, with Owen?"

Alys shrugged it off.

"We're friends, that's all."

Rhys glanced sideways at her. She could sense he wasn't buying it.

She stopped, even though they were still only halfway up the hill.

"Okay, he likes me. I like him too. But, I'm not into a casual thing and I'm not sure if Owen's up for anything else."

Rhys put his arm around her and squeezed her shoulder lightly.

"The man's a fanny magnet," she joked through the sadness she sensed that Rhys felt within her too. "And he's travelling so much, and I'm here not in Paris anymore. It's probably not gonna work out."

"Alys, stop putting up all the reasons why it won't work. Keep an open mind. Owen's always had women around him, that's true. But something tells me you're different. Give him a chance. And if anyone can figure out a way for you to be together, Owen can."

Reaching the cliff-top car park of La Galloise, Alys and Rhys gazed out to the sea and the islands beyond.

Maybe she would take a chance on him. But not for one night. She'd only have Owen if she could claim him as her own.

Back at party central, it was Mad Friday. The last Friday before Christmas, the start of the holiday season. And The Lobster Pot was bouncing.

The hardcore works' parties were out and they were going for it, and then some. One shirtless reveller was on top of the table doing a full-on Beyoncé booty shake as the waiting-on staff tried to pick their moment to clear the plates away.

By nine-thirty, Beth had run out of tequila and Jägermeister and the table of teachers in the corner had started a mince pie fight.

"God spare me from Christmas!" Alys sighed as she mopped up

another spilled pint of beer by the bar, the trills and licks of Mariah Carey piercing her brain yet again. It was all hands on deck. And with live music in the back bar, they'd be going until the wee hours.

Beth had booked an ABBA tribute band, who'd turned up as a twosome. A beard was Benny's only point of similarity and Agnetha was drawing a pension. Her white flared jumpsuit was threatening to split up the arse at any moment. Still, the party tables liked it, and at least they weren't singing Christmas songs.

Alys hopped on the bar to give Beth a hand to serve the scrum of people in front of them.

"What's happened to the other two?"

"Artistic differences," Beth said, taking a note to the till. "Anni-Frid's now an Amy Winehouse tribute act and Bjorn's gone to be her Blake. It was too late to cancel."

Owen was out too. He was in Cardiff with his old rugby mates. She had no idea what he was up to, but if it was anything like this lot, it was going to be messy.

Rugby was renowned for its hard-drinking culture, and although elite players like Owen weren't part of that scene, the gruesome stories she'd heard of rugby boy antics sent shivers down Alys' spine. It was meant to be a sport.

It was late. Way past the early hours, when her phone went off. Alys was still trying to clear the bar of the last of the revellers.

"Alys," he slurred on the video chat.

Owen was in a club. He looked dishevelled and very drunk.

She, on the other hand, was stone-cold sober.

"Alys, cariad. I need to tell you something."

Cariad? That was a new one. The Welsh word for love. A word reserved for parents speaking to their kids. For lovers.

"Can it keep 'til the morning? I can't hear you very well."

"I love you and I wanna fuck you, Alys. I'm not proud, I'll beg. Just say the word. Alys..."

He was gone.

He'd regret this, she smirked. If he claimed to remember it.

She put her phone into her trouser pocket. What was she going to do with that one? He was going to have a very sore head when he woke up.

She picked up more empty glasses from the beer-puddled tables.

Shit! He was meant to be making the first plane out to Paris for the match that afternoon. He'd need to be at the airport in a couple of hours. She hoped he'd make it. And that in the state he was in, they'd let him board the plane.

It was all over the Wales online news the next morning. She'd got up late, but couldn't believe what she was reading as she clicked on the trending story.

Owen Morgan, rugby international, snapped coming out of a club with a Britney Bevan, star of Barry Beach, a reality television show.

One moment he's swearing his undying love and lust for her. The next he's coming out of a club with a raven-haired, glamour model, with what looked like a pair of seriously enhanced breasts. How could he do that?

She felt sick. This was way worse than Leo.

Well, that was that, she decided determinedly. There was no way she was going there now with Mr Shallow. He could *do* one.

What had she been thinking anyway? Had she really believed that Owen Morgan would ever have committed to her? She'd been right all along. Friends or Fuckbuddies. That was the choice. It was her that had tried to mix it up. Suddenly, she couldn't wait for Christmas. To be at home with her folks again.

She padded downstairs through the lounge where one of their cleaners was vacuuming up the detritus of crackers, party-popper strings and mince pie crumbs littering the floor. The place smelled of hops, and her slippers were sticky from the spilled drinks that had soaked into the carpet.

She went through to the kitchen where Paul was checking

stock and getting a list together of things he needed for to-night's service. It was a much quieter evening, and more family-oriented now that the works' parties were over.

He looked at her chirpily.

"What's up, Missy? Were you joining in the celebrations last night?"

"I wish."

"So, why the long face?"

"Ahh, nothing... Men."

Paul put his arm around her and guided her to the kitchen stool where he'd been sitting.

He moved his lists out of the way and made them a coffee as she propped her elbows on the stainless steel prep bench and held her head in her hands.

"Come on. Tell your Uncle Paul all about it."

He grabbed another stool and sat down beside her with their coffees.

"It's Owen."

She frowned and sipped the coffee he'd put in front of her.

"We're friends, but there's a bit more between us too. He held me all night when I was having one of my nightmares," she rambled, unsure if Paul understood. "And we talk every day, and I thought he liked me. And then I wake up this morning and there's this photo of him coming out of a club with a glamour model. Some Britney from Barry?"

"Off the telly?"

"You know her?"

"Barry Beach. Sam watches it."

Alys shrugged.

"It's my fault. He told me he didn't do commitment. He told me that. And I still fell for him. Idiot that I am."

Paul put his arm around her.

"You're not the first, sweetheart. Tell me more about these nightmares."

CHAPTER 13

---------*---------

T he first snow was beginning to fall with large, wet flakes dissolving into the sea.

Alys looked up. The skies were like a blanket, the oppressive clouds were tinged a faint yellow. It felt expectant. Heavy.

The weather forecast had warned of snow. And whilst they never had as much on the coast, she had a three-hour drive through the hills before crossing the bridge over to her parents on the island of Anglesey.

The Lobster Pot was closed Christmas Day. She was sure Beth wouldn't mind her going a day early. She didn't fancy skidding her way up the lanes once the snow began to fall.

It was the twenty-third of December, after all. The big Christmas parties were now well and truly over. There were no more turkeys to be cooked. No more crackers to be pulled. And last night, still in a foul mood about Owen, she'd finally lost it. She'd snapped the Hundred Hits of Christmas CD in half and flung it in the bin. There'd be no more Mariah Carey. At least for another year.

"Paul," she called, as she headed back to the kitchen.

"I'm gonna give Beth a call. See if I can head off early for home. The snow's coming in and if I leave it till tomorrow I might struggle on the minor roads."

Paul came through.

"You're right. The forecast's bad. You take care, Alys. Take a flask and some food with you, and something to dig yourself out with."

"I'm sure Old Faithful will get me there."

She was borrowing Beth's ancient beat-up Toyota. She hoped that it would live up to its name."

"I thought you were seeing Owen today?"

She shrugged.

"If you see him, tell him I've gone home. I'll catch up with him in the new year."

Charles de Gaulle airport was busy. Travellers commandeered seats, lying across them, hunkering down. Knowing that their delayed flight wasn't leaving any time soon.

The boards kept changing. More and more flights were turning red. The delays and cancellations were increasing as a band of heavy snow swept down from the Arctic into mainland Europe.

Owen kept checking the board. So far, Bristol airport was holding clear. His stomach was churning, and he was feeling sick. He'd never been so anxious to get home. He couldn't wait to see her. They'd talked every day, but he'd still missed her not being around.

He tried a video chat, while he waited. There was no response. She must be working, he guessed. Preparing for the Saturday service.

He'd soon be there. He'd get the train from Bristol to Cardiff, grab the car and then head straight out of the city for the two-hour drive to Freshwater Bay. He'd be there by early evening if, fingers crossed, his flight on that board stayed green.

It'd been a mad couple of days. What had he been thinking, going out on a bender with the boys the night before the Paris match? Staying out all night and then flying back drunk as a skunk.

Luckily, the coach hadn't twigged or he'd have been fined. Or kicked out. No. Probably fined.

"Hey, Beth. Happy Christmas!"

Owen breezed into the lounge of The Lobster Pot as she was about to close up.

Seeing Owen, she came out from behind the bar and gave him a warm hug.

"How was your journey?"

"Long and slippery."

He nodded at her bump.

"You're looking great!"

"Thanks. We're still in shock."

"I thought you were a planner?"

"And me. I still am."

She ran her hand over her belly.

"Hey, but I'm learning that some surprises are cool too."

"Is Alys around?"

He strolled towards the kitchen, trying to play it casual in front of Beth.

"Owen, right? I'm Paul."

The chef came out of the kitchen door to shake his hand.

"Hi, Paul. Good to meet you. Have you seen Alys?"

"Uh, she's gone back to Anglesey. Went this morning 'cos of the snow."

Owen's face dropped. Why hadn't she waited for him? He'd have driven her through the snow. Had he misread the signs? Was she not bothered about meeting up with him?

"You got a sec?"

Paul guided him out of the bar and over to a table.

Owen followed him, more than a little antsy. The chef probably wanted tickets off him to one of the international games. It happened.

And he wasn't in the mood for a fan chat. He wanted to call Alys. Get back on the road and go up there tonight. Meet her folks. But, he didn't want to be rude. So, he sat down.

This Paul was staring at him. He wasn't much of a conversationalist. Owen cleared his throat, wanting him to get on with it.

"Look, Owen, she saw the photo of you, trending online."

"What photo?"

He wasn't sure he had ever trended. Even the time he scored a try against the All Blacks.

"You were papped coming out of a club. With a woman."

"As in Paparazzi?"

Owen got his phone out and googled himself.

There, on the screen, was a picture of him off his face with a girl draped all over him.

"She was in front of me, coming out of the club. She grabbed me."

"Alys doesn't think that...?"

Paul's eyes confirmed the worst.

He'd been trying her number last night and again this morning, but she'd still not picked up.

His mam was going to throw a wobbly when he told her. But he'd rather suffer her wrath than risk losing Alys.

Taking a deep breath, he took his bag and Christmas presents down the stairs and went to find his mother.

Ellen was in the living room cleaning out the ashes and laying up the fire.

He placed the presents under the Christmas tree.

"Those look interesting."

Owen turned to her.

"Mam, I've gotta go somewhere and I might not be back for Christmas Day. D'you mind?"

"What is it, son?"

"I have to see Alys."

She raised an eyebrow at that.

"What? In the Lobster Pot?"

"No. In Anglesey. She's gone home for Christmas."

"Owen, take a look outside."

He went to the window. It had been snowing hard when he got there last night, but by now everything was covered in a thick, deep blanket of white.

There were one or two tracks of yellow-edged footprints over a foot deep in the snow where Madog and David had been out that morning, feeding the animals and milking the cows.

"What's it like up north?"

"Worse. The main roads are passable but lots of the side roads are blocked. And everywhere's icy."

He rubbed his chin as he tried to work out his next moves. His sports car wasn't going to handle snow like that. And all the farm vehicles were needed here. He didn't have many options but to keep trying her phone.

Twenty-nine missed calls.

Alys' phone battery had died, and she'd only just plugged it in.

"Owen," she answered flatly as he appeared on screen. "What's wrong?"

"Alys, you've got to believe me. I had no idea."

He looked put out, upset even.

"What? You're not making sense."

"The picture of me, coming out of the club."

Her mouth twitched.

"Oh that. Have you been talking to Paul?"

"No... Okay... Yes. I have. He told me."

"It doesn't matter, Owen. I already know what you're like. We're only mates, remember?"

He looked at her intensely. His blue eyes shining through the screen.

"Is that right?"

"Yes," she breathed. "Just mates."

"Does it make any difference if I told you she pulled me in for the snap. Ten seconds later and I was in a taxi to the airport. I didn't go with her. I never would. Not now. Not ever. In fact, I haven't been with anyone, since before the wedding."

She cast her mind back with some surprise.

"But, that was October?"

"Tell me about it."

"What about Fanny?"

"One date in a bar. Her English wasn't that great."

"And Greta?"

"Never showed up."

Alys looked at him, her mouth curling at the edges.

"She didn't?"

"No. And, in case you ask, I had coq au vin for one that night."

"But you said…"

"No, *you* did. I just didn't correct you."

She flicked her hair back out of her face.

"So… things don't always work out for you, then?"

"No, things don't always work out. The snow's too bad. I can't see you over Christmas and I'm gutted."

"Me too."

Her confession slipped out and his face broke into a smirk.

"I'm hoping my luck will change by New Year."

CHAPTER 14

--------- ✸ ---------

Paul was off work and waiting for Vanessa at a table in the lounge of The Lobster Pot. He was early.

His boys, Sam and Dan, were both out in the back bar. Dan was catching up with his old school friends and Sam was hoping that his fake ID card would hold and that he'd get served, although Paul had already given the bar staff a heads-up.

It was Christmas Eve and there was a good crowd in the lounge bar. Most were in wellies and big coats and had walked there. The roads were covered in treacherous black ice.

"Did you manage to get hold of her?" Paul asked as Owen came in.

"Thanks, Paul. Yeah, I did. I got snapped with a random woman and it went viral."

"It happens," Paul said wryly. It had never happened to him.

"Can I ask you a question?" Paul broached.

"Sure. Fire away."

"Alys. She told me about her nightmares. And that you're helping her?"

"Uh, yeah... We've been doing some work on visualisation. Talking through what happened that night and in the dreams. Picturing positive scenarios to help her get out of the fire. A fire escape... a door..."

"A fireman?"

"Ha! I haven't suggested that. I don't want her dreaming of anyone else."

Paul stared at him. His face suddenly serious.

"Can you help me?"

Christmas night was always so tedious, Alys thought, bored out of her skull. Downstairs, her mother was glued to the hour-long Christmas soap special, and her dad was snoring. A large tumbler glass with a small remnant of whisky sat on the table beside his armchair. She'd forgotten how brain-numbing it could be at home. It was worse because she was an only child.

Upstairs, her room was exactly the same as it was when she'd left home. A shocking pink wall with a big daisy canvas in the centre. A pink patterned duvet covered her single bed. It was like she was still twelve. Like they'd refused to admit that she'd grown up and gone.

Powering up her phone she called Owen. Then, cringed with embarrassment as her phone screen filled with a sofa full of people.

He was in the lounge at the farmhouse. What was he playing at, answering her call in front of them all?

Her stomach flipped. Owen didn't do stuff like that by mistake. It was an announcement.

She wished she could be there. See him properly. Find out what was going on between them.

"Hey everyone, it's Alys," she heard him say.

A loud chorus of 'Happy Christmas!' sang out from the phone as Owen panned it around and everyone, in turn, waved at her.

They were having more fun than she was. There was his brother Madog and little Jake, his parents David and Ellen. Rhys and Ariana were there too. And Gareth and Beth, standing behind the sofa. Finn was asleep in Beth's arms.

Jake was about to flake out too. He was lying on his dad's chest, absently twirling his hair and sucking his thumb.

Owen moved out of the lounge into the darkened kitchen.

"That's better," he said sitting at the kitchen table. "It's chaos in there. Happy Christmas, Alys!"

"Happy Christmas!"

"Had a good day?"

"It was okay. Nice to see mam and dad," she answered.

"I missed you."

"You did?"

Her heart raced.

"I got you a present," he continued.

"What is it?"

"A surprise. You can open it New Year."

"That's not fair. You've gotta give me a clue. Is it like a perfume bottle shaped surprise?"

"More like a rugby ball shaped surprise."

"You got me tickets to a match?"

"No, I've got you some shin pads and a gum shield. Thought you might like to have a go now that you're Miss Fitness. Are you still running?"

"Every day, come rain or snow," she beamed. "I've got you a surprise too."

"A cookery shaped one?" he guessed. "Your chocolate mousse gateau?"

"No. I got you one of those aprons you found so amusing in Paris."

"What? The one with the naked woman on it?"

"Nah. The male one. The dude with the huge-"

His eyes smiled wickedly at her.

"What?" she carried on. "Beer belly and moobs, I was gonna say. That'll be you after you've eaten all my cakes."

"Alys?"

"Yeah?"

"I like it that you're still thinking about my body."

Vanessa snuggled into Paul's shoulder as they lay in front of the fire, in bathrobes. Two glasses of red wine on the low table in front of them.

He'd made her the most succulent harissa lamb dish with green beans and braised red cabbage, with an almond and pear tart dessert, eaten after a steamy session in the bedroom. The man was a machine. And he was seriously impacting on her waistline.

It was cold out. The snow was still piled in a slushy heap where it had been shovelled up the day before. Another week or so and she'd be warm and dry in Laos. After growing up working outside, moving from place to place with the circus, she hated the cold, wet British winters.

Paul squirmed.

"Vanessa, sweetheart, I'd better be going soon."

He kissed her hair as she gave a small sniff.

"What's wrong?"

"Nothing."

She couldn't say more, but this love-me-and-love-me arrangement, they had was cutting her up. She was sure she didn't snore. She didn't hog the bed. He didn't want the intimacy of sleeping with her. Just the sex.

"Aww, honey. What's up?"

She couldn't hold it in any longer.

"What's wrong with me that you never wanna stay?"

He paused and looked at her uncertainly.

"It's not you," he rasped. "It's me... My past."

"I don't understand."

He took a deep breath.

"I have awful night terrors."

She rotated around and gazed up at him.

"I'm afraid of you seeing them. And that I might hurt you. That night in Caernarfon, I stayed awake all night."

"Me too."

She tried to lift the mood. It couldn't be that bad.

He read her mind.

"I can be loud. I sweat. Thrash about."

"Shush... don't worry, love. Tell me what they're about."

He went through it all. He hadn't intended to. Not tonight. But once he started there was no stopping him.

He told her about Sangin. The Explosion. The debris. The betrayal. He explained how, in shock, he'd got himself up and ran over to the two boys. Picking up a leg here and an arm there, he'd tried to make the young men whole again. Until he couldn't do it, and then he'd collapsed and cried like a baby. Another para found him hunched into a ball on the ground. He had no memory of how they got him out of there.

Paul had talked it through with Owen. To be fair, he'd given his afternoon up on Christmas Eve to listen to Paul. Burying the trauma was the worst thing, Owen had told him. He needed to talk about it. In therapy.

Paul had blagged the army psych test after the attack. He'd gotten straight back into the fray. In active duty. That had been a mistake.

And Owen was right. It felt good, being able to tell Vanessa. Not easy. But good to share it.

The mental wounds were carved deep. There was no easy fix for his nightmares. No doorway, fire escape or even fireman here. His night terrors centred on his helplessness and guilt at not being able to save those boys. It tortured his waking mind every day, and it came out in his dreams.

Vanessa listened and said nothing. When he was done, she kissed him tenderly.

She wanted to tell him too, but now was not the right time. She took his hand and led him upstairs to her bedroom.

"V, after everything I've said. You still want me to stay?"

"Shush. 'Course I do. And I'm gonna take care of you all night," she whispered, pulling him down to her.

"Even now you know what you're getting into?"

She nodded guiltily. He didn't have a clue what he was getting into with her.

CHAPTER 15

---------*---------

"Oooh, it looks like we've got an accommodation booking for the next three nights." Alys looked up from the memo pad on the reception desk. "I didn't think we were doing hotel guests yet?"

"We're not," Paul answered. "Let's see?"

Beth had written it down.

"She's scrawled that she wants the front double suite room. Does that word look like 'owner' to you?"

Alys peered at it. Beth's handwriting was shocking. She was sure she was dyslexic. Quite a lot of chefs she knew were.

"I think so," Alys agreed. "Guess we get to meet the new owner. Exciting."

"Wonder what he or she's like?" Paul speculated, "Probably some London investor trying to get a foothold on the coast."

"Perhaps they're foreign? Like a Russian oligarch or a tech billionaire?"

"An angel investor?"

"Or a Sheik?"

By the time they'd finished, Alys had convinced herself and everyone else in the kitchen that the Lobster Pot had been bought by a Saudi Prince.

The evening was getting busy. They'd created a special New Year's Eve menu and Beth was at full pelt running the staff front of house. So, their mystery guest managed to slip in through the door, unnoticed.

In the kitchen, with their heads down, Alys and Paul were flat out cooking and guiding their junior chefs through the ninety covers. All of whom were dining late to pace themselves for the New Year celebrations.

Owen was in no rush to go down to the bar. He knew how it would be, and he wanted to let Alys get on with her work without any distractions.

Beth had confirmed that Alys didn't know he was staying. And he'd been amused to hear the tall stories and gossip going around the village about the new owner. Someone in the shop had told him that the place had been bought by a Saudi prince. He'd been called a few things in his life but never that.

He sat in his room. His room. His hotel. And he looked out at his view. The dark shadows of sailboats in the harbour. And beyond them, the inky open sea.

How was he going to tackle his next moves with Alys? After all, he was the rugby playmaker, the strategist. He should be all over this.

He hoped she wouldn't sidestep him and kick him into touch again.

His stomach flipped. It was eleven-thirty.

He slipped down to the bar and whispered into Beth's ear.

Her face broke into a grin and she readily agreed.

He had a plan.

"Alys?" Beth called through to the kitchen. "The owner wants a portion of your chocolate mousse gateau. He's asked for you to bring it up to him personally in his suite. He wants it before midnight. He was very specific."

Alys, who was finishing scrubbing down, wasn't impressed. Everything had been put away and cleared down so that they'd get out of there before the New Year countdown.

Going over to the fridge, she gave Beth a fake smile to her face and a sarcastic salute behind her back.

"The owner's always right," she chuntered, decorating the plate with chocolate swirls. She carefully placed the moussy gateau on it with a quenelle of cream on the top, a couple of raspberries and a sprig of mint.

Smoothing herself down, she went to check herself in the changing room mirror. She didn't look too bad, considering they'd done nearly a hundred three-course meals.

Holding the plate, she made her way up the back stairs to the first-floor suite.

What would he be like, she wondered? A fat middle-aged businessman, probably. Or a mysterious Middle Eastern sharp-suited tycoon. Probably not that Saudi prince, they'd imagined, though someone behind the bar had told Paul they'd seen a car full of men in suits in the village. His personal security team.

Holding the plate in one hand, she gave the door a knock.

A couple of seconds later, it opened wide.

But there was no one there.

She edged forward. Through the door, holding the plate high, her hand underneath.

"Good evening, Sir. I've your dessert for you."

Nervously, she stepped into the room.

"Alys."

"*Aargh!*"

Flinging her hands upwards, she twisted around to see Owen behind her by the door.

Too late. She shrieked as she sent the plate spinning off her hand like a discus through the air. Landing smack into him and splatting gateau mousse and cream all over his shirt and trousers.

Chewing her lip, she assessed the damage.

It was a sorry sight. She'd properly glooped him. His shirt and trousers were covered in a chocolate moussy mess.

"Oh my God! I'm so sorry. I thought you were a Saudi Prince. You gave me a fright."

Amused, Owen looked down at himself and began trying to scrape chocolate mousse and cream off his jeans, licking it off his fingers as Alys dashed to the bathroom.

Re-emerging a few seconds later with a wettened towel, she frantically began scraping the creamy chocolate off him, wiping him clean. Until she realised, with another shriek, that she was rubbing his crotch.

Owen raised an eyebrow and his lips curved mischievously as he teased her further by peeling off his shirt.

It worked.

Alys squealed again as her eyes glanced up in panic from his crotch and slammed straight into the wall of muscles that was his huge sculpted chest.

This was not how he'd envisaged it going at all. But he was really enjoying it.

Suddenly, a loud noise.

Alys gasped.

"What was that?"

Screams, whooping and popping carried up through the floor from the bar below.

He took her to him and held her by the shoulders. Steadying her. Calming her down.

She winced and took a long, deep breath. Dropping the towel to the floor.

"Alys. It's midnight. Happy New Year."

She gazed up into his eyes as he smiled at her disarmingly.

Drawing her to him and bending towards her, his mouth covered hers. It was the long, passionate, hot-mouthed kiss that he'd been dreaming about ever since she'd left him that Paris morning.

"Happy New Year," she breathed as they eventually moved apart.

Her face cracked into a contagious smile as they both assessed the state of his stained clothes and the chocolate mess around them.

He went over to his bag.

"Come and sit here with me," he directed her, gesturing to the seat pad on the big bay window. He had a small wrapped box, a present, in his hand.

Her eyes widened.

"For me?"

He nodded as her face lit up.

"I've got you a present too, but it's in my room,"

She shifted to go get it, but Owen stilled her.

"It'll keep until tomorrow."

She studied the wrapped box, shaking it to try and work out what it was.

"Hmm, a bit small for shin pads. Is it a gum shield?"

"Open it."

She flashed him a grin and started slowly tearing the corner and the paper away.

Inside the wrapping was a small carved wooden jewellery box.

"Thought we needed to create a new box, Alys. For us."

She glanced at him quizzically.

"So… not a fuckbuddy box?"

"No, Alys. Not a fuckbuddy box. Or even a friend box. How about, an I-want-you-to-be-my-girlfriend box?"

"You do?"

"Look inside."

She opened the box and took out two silver pendants, each on an expandable leather necklace cord.

He took one and she held the other in her hand.

"A Celtic swan," he said softly. "Put them together."

She held her swan to his, and they formed a perfect heart with their heads and necks.

She gazed up at him.

"It's… it's…"

"It's how I feel about you, Alys. You're right, this has slammed into me. I'm in new waters here with you. For the first time in my life, I find myself not wanting anyone else. Since I first saw you, it's always been you."

He slipped her necklace over her head, before placing a swan around his neck too.

"Owen, it's so beautiful."

She moved her mouth to his lips and kissed him again.

Owen responded, sliding his hand under her chef's jacket, feeling the bare skin of her waist.

She broke away suddenly.

"What if I screw this up, too? What if I've got it wrong?"

"What?" Owen rasped.

"I thought Leo was the one and that went sour real quick. What if this does the same?"

"Alys, stop worrying, will ya? Leo was an idiot. You're my best friend."

Her lips curled as she kissed him again.

"Owen, make love to me."

"You sure? Is that you begging me?" he whispered into her neck.

"Yes, " she answered breathily. "I'm begging. One of us had to."

Taking her hand, he rose up from the window seat and guided her across the room. Standing bare-chested with her at the end of the bed.

"I think things are a little uneven here."

Tugging at her white chef's jacket, the poppers gave way immediately. Her uniform fell to the floor revealing her full breasts barely cupped in black lace.

She exhaled nervously as his eyes slid over her.

He pulled her free of her trousers and released her hair from the tight bun that kept it away from food.

Laying her down flat on the bed, stripped to black lace, he gazed down at her. Taking in the sight of her smooth curvaceous body. Her hair fanned around the pillow as she lay beneath him.

"Alys, I will always dream of you like this."

He lay down beside her and kissed her, brushing her with fleeting kisses along her neck and down along her collarbone and the dip of her neck to her glorious breasts. He wanted to take it slow. Their first time. He wanted to make love to her.

Slipping his arm underneath her waist, he rolled her to him, undoing her bra single-handedly and blindly in one deft move.

"An expert."

"You have no idea yet," he mouthed into her ear. "Let me show you what I can do."

He started slowly. His hands and mouth edging in exploration towards those breasts he'd been dreaming about. And he lingered over them, paying them the attention they deserved. Taking them in his mouth, sucking, nuzzling and nipping at her nipples.

She bucked against him, the passion rising. Her fingers moved insistently around his waist, seeking the zipper on his fly, trying to unfasten his trousers and free him. To hurry up and take her fast. To take control.

But he held her back, keeping her simmering as her passion began to boil over. And began again.

This time, holding her arms playfully by the wrists above her head. Keeping her pinned as he worked his way down. Another time, he'd tie her with a scarf. She said she enjoyed that.

Holding her fast, moving his mouth southwards, she was helpless. Unable to do anything but succumb to his kisses. His tongue gliding over her stomach. His mouth working its way down, teasing her by missing exactly where she wanted him to focus.

"Keep your hands above your head," he instructed her as he released his grip and he took her foot. He nibbled the inside of her ankle.

She swept back her head, holding onto the pillow. Surrendering to him as he swept his way up to the back of her knee. And he felt her quivering in anticipation as his tongue feathered the inside of her thigh.

When he reached her panties, he pulled them off her with his teeth, pausing to kiss her. Making her moan.

"Hands," he reminded her as they slipped onto him.

She lifted them back above her head.

Now she was properly simmering with lust, he paid her full attention to where she desperately craved him. Expertly swirling his tongue over her core until she was thrumming with the orgasm that was building up inside her.

And when it came, it smashed into her hard. She cried out his name as she clenched tight around his fingers. Her hands broke free of their invisible ties, moving onto him. Her nails digging into his back.

"I want you inside me. Now."

"Miss Impatient. I say when."

He pinned her back to the bed with his body. His hand over her wrists.

He grinned as he felt her shiver.

Slowly moving off her, he stripped away his trousers and boxers as she watched on.

He reached for his wallet from his trouser back-pocket. He was sure he had one. So much for being the strategist. He had a packet in his washbag.

Her eyes widened as he stood in front of her. Naked and erect.

"Don't go anywhere, I gotta get a rubber from the bathroom."

"I'm on the pill," she whispered, moving herself up to kneel on the bed. She took his hands and pulled him back down to her. Then, flipping him flat she moved on top of him, kissing him insistently, feverishly until the flames of lust soared again in him too.

He tried to gain back control. But, moving slowly downward, she began exploring his body with her mouth, and he let go.

She sucked and nibbled his pectorals, feeling the ridges of his abs with her fingers, working her way thoroughly over his hard, muscular body until she had him in her mouth.

"Alys," he rasped. "If you carry on, I won't be able to stop, and I've never done it without a..."

"You're a virgin then," she teased as she slowly dragged her tongue over him, swirling over the tip.

"I just got checked. Clean as a whistle."

He exhaled shakily and pulled her up to him.

"Let me be your first," she said huskily, grazing her lips over his.
He kissed her deeply.

Then, moving her to straddle him, he pulled her down and pushed himself smoothly up into her.

She threw her head back and he kissed the length of her neck as he buried himself inside her, balls-deep. Drawing a jagged breath of exhilaration, he felt her deliciously tight, pressed against his bare skin for the very first time. She fitted him like a glove.

Slowly, she began moving with him as his hands stroked her waist and kneaded her breasts. Lifting himself, he sucked her nipples, then lay back as she pushed down on him again.

She rode him like a bucking bull. Letting him build the pace, following his lead as he moved her, pulling her up and pushing down faster and harder, faster and arching back to push him even deeper, accentuating his movements. Gripping him tight. Holding on. Until at last, she threw her head back, his name on her lips as she tightened around him.

Flipping her he pushed into her again, pumping her hard and shooting her back skywards. Following her lead, he rocketed too pulsing inside her as he fell apart.

Neither of them could move.

They lay together. Side-by-side. Holding hands. Their silver swans bobbing up and down to the rise and fall of their ragged breaths.

"My God, Alys. I knew we'd be good. But you... you're *frickin' fantastic*."

CHAPTER 16

--------- ✳ ---------

"**H**appy New Year, darling."
Paul cracked open the champagne that she'd left on ice.

It was one a.m. and he was just back from the Lobster Pot. Vanessa was meant to have been waiting up but she'd fallen asleep on the sofa and missed the New Year countdown.

Her hair was a little mussed up, and her eyes still woozy from her deep sleep. She would have secretly preferred a cup of tea to the champagne, but she took a sip from her glass to be sociable.

Paul, on the other hand, was buzzing. After working at full pelt all evening, he was in no hurry to sleep.

"I have a surprise for you. I hope you'll like it," he said a little nervously, getting his phone out.

"What is it?"

He scrolled through his phone and found the wallet app, holding it out in his hand for her to see.

"You're coming."

"Sorted it with Sam. He's fine. I put the fear of God into him, so I'm hoping the house'll not become a teenage party hangout."

"Oh, Paul. You'll love Laos. I'm so excited."

"I can only do January. While the Lobster Pot's shut."

Paul gazed into her eyes.

"I love you, Vanessa."

She flinched.

Paul's face looked pained.

It was confusing. He was the first man that she'd wanted in her life since she'd moved there. But, how could he say he loved her when he didn't know the first thing about her? About who she really was.

"You won't love me when you know everything."

She put a finger to his lips as he made to disagree.

"I'm gonna tell you it all. And, then you can decide if you do."

Her family was hard to explain. Unless you lived it, you didn't understand. The circus was a tough place. You grew up fast.

At fourteen, she'd fallen for one of the animal handlers. A rough type with a bed for the night in every town, Lee was ten years older than her. What should have been a teenage crush quickly developed into a full-blown affair.

"When the circus stopped, he took me to London. Got us married straight away so I couldn't leave him. It was me earning the money. I was seventeen when I started working in the club."

Her eyes met Paul's.

"Pole dancing. And the rest. You still wanna stay?"

He nodded but his face was stony.

She took a deep breath. If he walked away, it would be for the best. She'd been a victim, she hoped he understood. She had no room in her life for judgements about her past.

"He took all the money I made. He was keeping me safe, he said. Although he never stopped the men from touching me. He liked to watch. And he went with other women too."

"Honey, you don't need to..."

"I do."

She told him about Lee. The minder and her mindfuck who'd pimped her, and imprisoned her like the caged animals he'd kept so cruelly at the circus.

"He managed everything I did. Who I talked to. Where I went. He kept me in the flat most of the time. I could never make any decisions for myself. It's hard to describe, but I was young, Paul. He made me feel safe and cared for, but he was totally controlling and volatile. The hard drugs he was taking didn't help. They made him edgy. Paranoid."

"So, what's your real name?"

"Vanessa Kraft."

"Kraft?"

"Yeah. I changed it legally when I first moved here."

"And where's your ex-husband now?"

"Prison. For grievous bodily harm and drugs convictions. I've escaped from my past and spent the last five years building a new life. All on my own."

She rubbed his leg.

"I won't hold it against you if you wanna walk away?"

He caught her hand as it drifted up his thigh.

"V, how could I?"

She blew out a deep breath as he drew her hand to his lips.

"I'm proud of you," he said softly. "When I first saw you, it was your strength that drew me to you."

"Really?"

The emotions welling up, choking her voice.

"Yes. That and your cute butt in those tight jeans. Has anyone told you how great your arse is, by the way?"

"All that dancing," she smirked through the threatening tears. "I'm very flexible too."

A growl escaped his throat.

"Show me."

When Alys came to, it was well into New Year's Day.

Feeling those familiar, large arms around her, she cast her mind back to the night before, smiling smugly to herself as she felt the swan resting on her breastbone. It felt sensational being a sex goddess.

She couldn't believe it. She was now Owen Morgan's girlfriend. And he owned the Lobster Pot. Nothing much had been said the night before about that little snippet, they'd had other things on their mind.

Owen stirred and began nuzzling her ear.

She squirmed and felt him hard against her as she turned back into his arms and his huge wall of his chest.

"Come and get wet with me again."

Alys lightly brushed her lips over his, feeling the stubble on his face.

"I think the owner might need to renovate, that shower inside the bath thing needs remodelling. The soap dish on the side was halfway up my arse last night."

Owen smirked.

"I thought that was me."

He'd claimed every bit of her. Wow. She'd never come as hard as she had, so many times. The way he controlled her. Teased her and made her wait. It was glorious torture. Even if it didn't last, she'd always have the memory of her night with Owen Morgan.

She giggled as he blew onto her neck, rubbing his stubbly face over her, making her squeal.

"Hmm. Let's try that shower out again. Check how bad it is so you can write the owner a letter of complaint."

Alys pulled away.

"Does this mean you're my boss now?"

"No. But we've got to decide what we wanna do with this place."

"*We?*"

Owen rolled on top of her, propping himself up so he didn't crush her. Gazing steadily into her eyes.

"Yes. We. It's something we can do together. Turn it into a place we can be proud of. Once I finish playing rugby."

She wasn't sure what exactly he wanted to do, and Beth still had the lease. It was damned hard work. Did he really want to run a hotel?

He studied her face, trying to mind-read.

"We're a great team, Alys."

He kissed her, then whispered in her ear, "I've fallen in love with you."

She kissed him back.

Her heart was so full of love, but her head screamed out in panic. Was she being pulled headfirst into another disastrous whirlwind?

After she'd gone back to the owner's apartment for some fresh clothes, Alys met Owen by the harbour wall. They were both determined to get some fresh air and take a New Year's Day walk before the early afternoon dusk descended.

She held out her hand. She was carrying a small package, beautifully wrapped by Ariana.

"Your Christmas present."

Owen stared at it curiously.

"Too small for an apron."

"Yeah, and you had the chocolate mousse present last night."

He pulled open the paper and recognised the pouch. A signet ring dropped into his palm.

"It's a shield design," she told him. "For warriors."

Owen tried it on. It was a size too small.

She chewed her lip.

"Ariana said she'd adjust it."

"I love it, Alys. And I love you."

There he went again with those words.

He pulled her to him but she pushed him back with her palms.

"Owen."

He held her shoulders and then took both her hands. They felt warm. Lacing his fingers in hers, he gazed down at her.

"What are you scared of, cariad?"

She motioned with her head towards the white rambling building behind them.

"This. It's all too fast. I'm loving being your girlfriend. You're amazing. But, you owning The Lobster Pot? Saying you love me. It's got me in a tizz."

"Why?"

"I'm not sure what you want from me?"

He pulled her to him, circling his arms around her waist.

"I want you with me. Us together."

"Me too."

Owen exhaled, pleased.

"What about this, though? The Lobster Pot?" Alys pushed.

"For now, nothing. Until we decide what we want to do with it."

"There you go with the *we* again. What if *we* break up? What if you fall out of love with me, like Leo did?"

She'd said it.

"Alys, that's never gonna happen."

He kissed the tip of her nose.

"Okay. So, *I* might fall out of love with you."

"So, you do love me, then?"

He grinned, holding her gaze.

She coloured up. Mr Alpha was infuriating.

"You got me. Yes, I love you too, Owen."

She glanced away.

"That's the best Christmas present."

He brushed her cheek with his lips, drawing her to look at him again.

"Alys, you gotta take a risk. Once the international matches start, we won't see much of each other, unless you can get to Cardiff or Paris."

"That's not gonna be easy," she admitted.

"This place. It's where I wanna be longer term. For now, I need your help to think about what kinda hotel The Lobster Pot should be. I'm lucky, I've got the funds and it's a great investment. But there's no rush. I can keep leasing it to Beth. But, if you want a career break, this could be ours. Or not. I said we'd make a great team. I believe in you, Alys. I believe in us. Together."

"You do?"

"Uh-huh. There's something else too."

Taking her hand, they started walking from the harbour up the steep hill to La Galloise car park.

On the clifftop, they squinted as they faced out to sea and into the biting wind. It was whipping the waves into big white curls, making them dance across the bay. The islands beyond were hardly visible as a dark grey cloud had descended, obscuring the horizon.

"There's our new house."

She wasn't sure where he was pointing to. The only thing she saw was the boathouse tucked back into the rocks below.

"I bought it off Gareth last October."

Alys was stunned.

"I told you. I want to be here with you in Freshwater Bay."

CHAPTER 17

---------*---------

"**I** gotta go get breakfast. I love you, Alys."
"Love you too. Score one for me."
"I'll try my best. If I do, I'll send you a message."
The screen went black. Owen was gone.

He was at the team hotel preparing for the biggest game of the season, England versus Wales at Twickenham. The home of English rugby. It was always a grudge match, and England at Twickenham was the toughest gig of all.

They'd spent most of January inseparable while The Lobster Pot was closed. And Alys had moved with Owen between Cardiff and Paris, never spending a night apart. This relationship wasn't like the one she'd had with Leo. Their love, if anything, had deepened rather than cooled. They were so compatible in ways she'd had no idea about.

She knew he was an alpha when they'd met. It was what had attracted her to him. But, she'd not understood the full implications of that. And boy, had he taught her some new moves. And things about herself, she'd never realised.

In the bedroom, she was totally at his mercy. No one had ever asked her for a safe word before. It was exciting and edgy. And he knew exactly how, where and when to push her over the edge. Again and again.

Being away from him hurt. He felt it too. The next few weeks were going to be tough. She was back full time at The Lobster Pot now February had arrived, and Owen was racing between his Paris club commitments and his Wales international games.

The national squad was run like a military camp and the team were in lockdown at their hotel for three days before each match, making it unlikely that they'd see each other much over the next six weeks. The odd Sunday in Cardiff and the daily video calls would be all they could manage for now.

Beth was at the boathouse, getting ready for her shift on the bar at the Lobster Pot. Even Gareth had been roped in to help serve drinks through the rugby game, with Ellen babysitting Finn.

England versus Wales. It was going to be dizzy-busy. She looked forward to getting back to being a restaurateur again. This pub business wasn't her bag, at all.

Gareth's mouth dropped open as she came down the stairs.

"You can't wear that."

His face was filled with horror.

"Why not?"

She straightened the collar on her white England rugby shirt.

"'Cos, *A*, you'll get lynched, *B*, we'll lose all our customers and *C*..."

"What's *C*?"

"*C* is, that when Wales win you'll get the shit ripped out of you for weeks."

He pulled open a drawer by the kitchen island and took out a plastic bag.

"I got you this. It's for the best."

She peered into the bag and reluctantly pulled out the red Wales shirt.

"OK," she huffed. "I'll do it... For you. But, I can't promise I won't cheer when England scores."

It was half an hour before kick-off, and Rhys and Ariana had saved Alys a seat around the table with them, in front of the large television screen in the Lobster Pot lounge bar.

Ariana had been having a few pains that morning. She wasn't sure if this was it, or whether they were Braxton Hicks. Rhys' car was in the car park with a bag packed, just in case.

Ariana handed Alys the adjusted signet ring. She'd give it to Owen when she saw him in Cardiff in a fortnight's time. She couldn't wait until then. She'd bought a black basque and a couple of other items for them to try. Owen Morgan was turning her into a wickedly adventurous sex slave.

"How are Gwen and Ed enjoying their big trip?" Alys asked Ariana.

"Having a whale of a time. They're in Australia now. They've been swimming on the Great Barrier Reef."

Rhys chipped in.

"Mam's been pushing brochures under Dad's nose. Thinks it's time they did a trip too. David's got a cousin farming in the South Island of New Zealand that they've always wanted to visit."

The bar was filling up.

Paul, back from Laos, appeared from the kitchen to check how busy they were. He pulled a face when he saw the size of the scrum trying to get served and dived in to help Beth and Gareth.

He quirked an eyebrow at Beth's red rugby shirt.

"Traitor."

"Coward," she taunted back as he flashed her a peak of his England shirt hidden beneath his chef whites.

By now, the bar was a loud sea of red shirts, laughing, joking and drinking. Every table was covered in amber glasses of beer and the crowd was getting rowdy, with people either clambering at the bar for a drink or standing around the big screens, watching and waiting.

Shhhh.

The bar noise hushed to a whisper, as on the screen the players came out of the tunnel and lined up in the middle of the pitch for the anthems prior to the start of play.

The camera tracked in an upshot along the line of players. White, then red. The brass band began, and the bar joined the stadium crowd, bursting into the melodic harmonies of the Welsh National Anthem.

The camera tracked again along the players, with close-ups on each face. All of them had their fists on their hearts, eyes staring ahead. In the zone.

The bar cheered as Owen came into shot.

A thick Welsh voice cut through the crowd as the singing died down.

"Absolute legend."

The local lad was wearing his country's colours again.

Twickenham erupted as the egg-shaped ball was kicked high into the air, marking the opening of the game.

Echoes of 'Swing Low Sweet Chariot' reverberated around the England stadium. And in the bar of this little corner of Wales, a rowdy rendition of where 'said chariots' could be stuck, was enthusiastically sung back at them.

Gareth gave Beth a told-you-so look. She'd made the right decision to go red.

The game was a tetchy affair. The weight of the England pack meant that they were going for a scrummage game, with their heavy forwards making rolling mauls towards the try line. Wales defended, again and again. A line of red pushing back against the brutal, battering whites.

Alys winced as she saw Owen take a heavy shoulder charge. But he overpowered his opponent, holding his man down firmly until the England player collapsed flat.

Holding on to the ball. Advantage Wales.

But, nothing came of it.

England put pressure on again with waves of attack. The line of red was still holding. Strong and impenetrable.

Then, finally, a fleeting chance. A missed pass from England five metres off the Welsh try line was dramatically intercepted by Owen. In a split second, he'd found a winger with space to his left and he passed the ball to him out wide.

The winger caught the pass one-handed in the air. Tucking the ball safely under his arm he raced away, sprinting for his life down the side-line into space. Running blisteringly fast, side-stepping to change his lines, running clear.

The winger was now three-quarters of the way down the pitch with only a couple of white shirts half-heartedly jogging after him.

The redshirted stadium supporters roared. A whole nation was screaming. And the bar erupted.

"GO ON!!!"

Dropping the ball sweetly straight in front of the posts, Owen and the number eleven embraced in joyful triumph.

Five points to Wales and an easy conversion through the goalposts made it seven.

"*YESSSS!!!*"

Cheering, followed by a loud round of 'Hymns and Arias,' bounced around the bar.

Rhys hugged Ariana, then Alys, and shook hands with random people who kept coming up to him, congratulating him. His brother, the playmaker, had made the try.

The camera focussed on Owen as he jogged back for the restart of play. Glancing up, he saw himself close up on the big stadium screen and made a heart with his hands.

Alys blushed. That was for her.

Gareth patted Beth's rear as he shimmied past her on the bar to pour another Guinness.

"You picked the right team."

"Okay, I give in. I'm officially adopted. I'll support the reds."

The game carried on, evenly matched. England won back two penalties making Wales one point ahead at half time. The score, six to England seven to Wales.

Both teams came back on in the Second Half fired up and ready to take control of the game. Wales had the ball and were moving from halfway towards the England twenty-two line.

They were in phases of play. Pick and chase. Wales pushing forward, England tackling the player down. Wales reforming and passing the ball back out from behind for the centre to pass to the next.

Again. And then again.

Owen picked up the ball and hammered himself forward into the English defensive line.

Snap.

The agony was instant as he was suddenly, violently tackled down from behind.

In unison, the bar gasped. A stunned silence, no one quite believing what they'd seen, followed by angry shouts of foul play.

It was horrific. Rhys covered his eyes and grabbed the back of his neck in disbelief as he watched the gruesome replay. Alys had blanched a pallid shade of grey.

Owen's leg could clearly be seen bending above his ankle, snapping flat to the ground.

He was now lying in agony on the grass with a circle of players around him.

It was serious. An England player had kicked the ball out of play and the bibbed medical team were racing on. There was no quibble, the stretcher was there in the field with them too.

Gareth pushed through the crowd towards Rhys.

"Did I see that right?"

Rhys' eyes were glued to the screen, his hands now holding Alys' and Ariana's tightly.

"It's a bad break," Rhys confirmed. "The stretcher's on and they're giving him oxygen. Definitely a hospital job, I'd say they'll be putting in a pin."

The whole stadium, white and red, stood and clapped in respect as Owen, writhing in pain, was stretchered off the field. His face was covered in the oxygen mask, his leg concealed with a blanket from view.

Alys looked to Gareth in horror.

"What happens next?"

"They'll call Dad. Give him an update later, once they get him to the hospital. Best case scenario, he's out for the season."

"Worst case?"

Gareth didn't answer. No one had said it yet, but it would probably be the last professional match that Owen Morgan ever played.

The match ended thirteen, ten to England. Wales had lost, but Alys didn't notice. All she could do was wait anxiously for news after the team doctor had called the farm.

David, Owen's father, took the phone call later that evening. Owen was back in Cardiff, undergoing surgery. A metal rod was being screwed in to help repair his snapped tibia and fibula bones.

Whilst Owen was having surgery, Rhys and Ariana were having their own drama. Her water broke as she walked across the Lobster Pot car park to the car. Their baby was on its way.

CHAPTER 18

----------*----------

Knocking on the door, Alys gingerly entered the private hospital room where Owen was recovering. Before she'd gone in, one of the nurses had warned her not to expect too much from him.

He was dressed in a t-shirt and shorts, lying on the bed. His injured leg was flat and braced in a round cage that surrounded him from the knee down. His eyes stared up towards the ceiling and he barely turned to glance at her as she entered the room.

She stared at the gruesome open wound. The break had created what they called an open fracture. The nurse said he'd only be allowed home once there was no risk of infection.

After that, he'd have to keep it dry and clean. And when the frame was removed, there'd be a brace or a boot. The healing process stretched ahead of him for a good few months. The rest of this season was certainly wiped out. And probably much more.

"Owen, I'm so sorry."

Still fixed on the ceiling, he opened his arms to her as she leaned over him. He was blinking back his tears as she covered him with light kisses.

Her head rested on his chest as she scooted onto the bed beside him.

"It's all over, Alys," he murmured.

"Shush, no one's said that yet, Owen."

"What am I gonna do?"

She craned her neck and stretched up to find his lips.

"Let's work on getting you home and we'll take it from there, yeah?"

Shaking his head a fraction, he turned his head away from her. He was back to staring at the ceiling.

When Owen finally rolled his wheelchair through the door into his Cardiff apartment, the vases of flowers and gifts from well-wishers and colleagues from across the rugby world overwhelmed him.

But it wasn't their kindness that made him emotional. The cards and kind words only confirmed the worst. His playing days were over.

Beth had given Alys time off to care for Owen in Cardiff once he was discharged. His leg had to stay elevated to reduce any swelling and he could only get about in a wheelchair or on crutches. No driving allowed.

The risk of infection was the biggest concern, and he was reliant on Alys to do the simplest of tasks.

It was humiliating. He was like a baby. She even had to help him wash and dress, go to the bathroom, the toilet.

Alys said she didn't mind. She fed him. She took him to appointments, shopped, did the housework, took the calls. She was his P.A., sorting the Paris apartment and organising for his things to be packed and sent to Cardiff. She'd frozen down meals in batches for him, for when she had to go back to work.

Alys had been an absolute trooper. And he couldn't bear it. Or the concern and pity in her eyes. He was a cripple. Not even a quarter of the man he was.

Depressed, and wanting to be alone, he spent most of his time laid flat in his bed. The door closed. His leg elevated. Alys banished to the spare room.

She tried him with books. His laptop. A television. But he spent most of his first few days sleeping or staring into space. She tried sitting with him and chatting. But he was quiet and sulky. She'd put on a film, but he'd slowly drift into his own thoughts, soon losing interest.

She even turned up one time in the bedroom wearing the sexiest black basque. And he'd made her cry when he'd turned his head away and refused to look at her.

She called him a self-absorbed bastard as she slammed the door behind her. And she was right. He was. But she didn't get it. The bottom had fallen out of his world. He would never play rugby again.

"I don't know what else I can do," Alys levelled with Rhys over the phone as she wandered along the waterfront in Cardiff Bay.

Cooped up in that apartment was turning her stir-crazy. Owen was impossible. She couldn't break through to him. And worse than that, he didn't love her anymore. Or fancy her.

Before, if she'd have put that basque on, he'd have gone crazy for her. What had happened to them? He'd broken his leg, and broken her heart.

"He's been out of hospital two weeks, he should be getting better."

"He sounds depressed," Rhys suggested.

"I think so too. But it's like talking to the wall. What if I'm making it worse? Perhaps it's best if I go?"

"Don't be silly, Alys. Owen puts on this confident image, like he's some alpha male athlete. But, deep-down he's as lost as the rest of us. This is massive for him. His whole world's gone."

"Hmm. Including me, if he carries on," she deliberated grimly.

"We'll come over."

"No, Rhys. You've enough on your plate, with Nansi."

"We'll bring her too. She's been wanting to meet her Uncle Owen, anyway. She told me this morning."

A laugh escaped her lips.

"You sure?"

"Yep. See you tomorrow."

She turned back towards the waterfront. She'd buy a coffee, read a magazine. Anything, to stay away a bit longer and avoid going back to more cold shoulders and rejection from the man she couldn't help but love.

Alys was dressed for a run when Rhys and Ariana arrived at the Cardiff apartment the next day with a car seat carefully carried in by Rhys.

"Ohhh," Alys cooed, looking at the little face popping out of the baby blanket she was tucked up in.

"Meet Nansi."

Ariana scooped the tiny baby out of the seat and cradled her in her arms for Alys to see.

Nansi was the prettiest little baby, with a mop of thick black hair and big, bright blue eyes.

"She's so beautiful."

"Like her mother."

Ariana rolled her eyes.

"And you're just like your brother," Alys added. "Very smooth."

The girls decided on going for a coffee. Rhys insisted on taking full charge of Nansi.

"Thank you," Alys mouthed silently to Rhys as they left.

Inside Owen's apartment, Rhys made them both a coffee, whilst Owen took Nansi into his huge hands. She lay quietly, staring up at him.

"You and me, we're about as helpless as each other," he whispered, cradling his new baby niece gently in his arms.

He studied the perfection of her tiny hands and fingernails. He'd never thought about that before. And he couldn't get over that his brother Rhys, who'd been so screwed up twelve months before, was now so settled. A married man with a new career. A father. It was the grain of hope, he'd been grappling to find.

"Owen," Rhys cut through the niceties. "Alys thinks you're depressed. I do too."

His eyes were still fixed on Nansi.

"She doesn't understand what I'm going through."

"No one does, Owen. Talk to me about it. Come on, bro. Tell me."

Rhys reached out to him as tears sprang up and rolled down the cheeks of the six-foot-five warrior.

Rhys gently took Nansi from him and set her back down in the baby seat.

Owen let out a ragged breath and wiped his face, embarrassed. But Rhys ignored that and drew his brother into a strong hug.

Owen let go.

"It's all gone, Rhys. I'm never going to be part of it again."

Rhys could feel his pain.

The big guy'd been bottling it up. Toughing it out, playing the hard man. And all the time he'd been hurting. Crying inside. Mourning for the loss of more than just his rugby career. It was who Owen Morgan was. The rugby player. And now his identity had been taken from him, who the Hell was he?

"You've so many things you can do next. Owen, look at me. Who'd have thought that this screw-up could do it?"

Owen nodded, his head still bowed.

"Don't shut Alys out. Your leg's the worst thing that's happened to you, but she's the best. Don't lose her too."

Owen looked up, a little shocked.

"Why? Has she said something?"

"No. But, it can't be easy for her."

"I've been a total arse to her."

"She can forgive you for that. You've been trying to get your head around it all. But it's been nearly a month now, Owen. You've gotta try and get over it, or it'll swamp you even more."

It wasn't as easy as flicking a switch. Suddenly making it right. How he felt, it was like a blackness consuming him. Making everything seem pointless.

But it was true. His life would never be the same again, and he had to learn to accept that. It happened to all players eventually. And he was no different. He'd had ten wonderful years at the top of his game. And now it was over.

"Talk to Alys. Let her in. This is one door shutting. But, heck, you've got ten others you can open. Most of us mere mortals only have one or two."

Owen gave him a weak smile. Rhys did have a point. With his connections and his academic studies, he had the potential to go in any number of different directions. And sitting, brooding, wasn't getting him anywhere. He always had a plan, whatever he did. And he needed one now.

"Thanks, bro. It means a lot to me that you came to see me today. Let me hold Nansi again."

Another tear escaped down the tough guy's cheek, and he sniffed back the others that threatened to follow as he held the baby girl in his arms.

When it was time for Rhys and Ariana to leave, he took her out of the flat and into the shared hallway.

"Hang on in there, okay."

She nodded bravely as she thanked them both for making the trip.

Owen stretched his arms out to her as she went back into the living room. She went over to him, unsure, but he hugged her for the longest time.

"I know it's not been easy," he mumbled into her hair.

His voice was thick. She hadn't noticed when she'd come in, but he was in tears.

"I am gonna try, Alys. I promise."

She let his head bury itself into her chest as she held him, like a child. She had no idea to mend him, help him with the pain he was going through. All she knew was that she would stay. She'd stay and be there for him, weathering his depression and his moods. She'd keep on trying to comfort him and help him out of the dark place he'd found himself in. She'd be there until he asked her to leave.

CHAPTER 19

---------✳---------

Vanessa was sure that her security lights had flicked on at around three am. It happened. Badgers, rabbits. It was like living on safari out here in West Wales. It was so different from London. Quiet and peaceful. That's what she loved the most.

So, when she left the house that morning she was appalled to see that someone had keyed the paintwork all along the side of her SUV, carving out a deep silver gouge.

Bastards. They'd done the whole side. It must have happened in town, the day before. In the supermarket or maybe at the leisure centre when she was teaching her yoga class? It had been dark when she drove back home, she wouldn't have noticed.

Paul came over to assess the damage and had a pretty similar reaction. It was irritating, but at least she was alright and it could be fixed.

"Best log it with the police," he agreed. "The re-spray's not gonna be cheap."

Paul was frustrated he couldn't do more. She bristled when he said she was too independent. He didn't get it. She was quite capable of phoning her insurance company to make a claim, she told him bluntly.

"Look, I'm coming over after work. I'll stay with you," he decided that evening over the phone.

"No. I'm fine," she snapped.

His tone riled her. It was up to her if she wanted him there. Not him. What was going to happen? The only recorded crime out where she lived was the squirrel stealing peanuts from the bird feeders.

"How about we have a bit of space for a night or two? Catch up on some sleep?" she suggested.

It wasn't meant to be a dig, but Paul took it that way. He went quiet on the other end of the line.

Two nights ago she'd seen his nightmare for the first time. He'd been terrified about it happening while she was with him. But it had, and she'd coped. She came to and saw him agitated, in REM, twitching and moaning. She'd held him in her arms, stroking him to try to calm him down as he'd woken up.

He was still a little touchy about it.

"If you're sure you'll be alright?"

"Absolutely," she said through gritted teeth. "I'll call you."

She was never going to be controlled by a man again.

Alys opened the door into Owen's apartment.

"That sounds interesting. I'll think it over and get back to you." Owen's voice carried through the living room into the hall.

It had been blowing a hoolie outside and the car park was full, so she'd had to park Owen's car on the street a fair distance away. He wasn't going to be pleased. That car was his baby. But she'd had no choice, she'd move it later.

Her hair was soaked and plastered to her face, her coat was dripping with rain, and she was juggling three bags of shopping, about to spill the bread and eggs all over the floor.

She was right. Owen was talking to someone in the apartment. There was a woman with him in the lounge.

She stumbled with the bags through to the kitchen, a soggy mess. She dropped the bags onto the kitchen counter.

Fantastic. In the lounge was his ex fuckbuddy, Julia.

And she was looking... dry. Polished, in fact. Glamorous and camera ready.

Her eyes flicked onto Alys who was now dripping puddles onto the carpet. Red-faced, dressed in holey leggings and wearing a baggy sweatshirt under her oversized waterproof.

She could tell that Julia was assessing her carefully, weighing up the minor assets and major flaws of Owen's new woman. Alys gave her a semi-polite smile and tried to make a dive for the bedroom.

"Julia. This is my girlfriend, Alys."

Good on him. Owen was laying it out to Julia. But, *really!* Did she have to face her nemesis at this precise moment?

Julia gave Alys a broad television presenter smile and stretched her hand out confidently, brazenly even, Alys thought.

And Owen was perky. That didn't help Alys' mood, either. In fact, it only made her even more jealous as Julia openly flirted with him.

She didn't like Julia being in the apartment. It made her think of them both together, before her. Here. In his bed. They'd been in the middle of a deep conversation together before she walked in. And they were having a private conversation again, now as she went to put the groceries away.

Thankfully, Julia didn't stay long. When Alys emerged from the bedroom in fresh tidier clothes, Julia quickly made her excuses about getting the train back to London.

"Phone me, yeah?"

She laid her hand provocatively on Owen's shoulder, her fingers lingering on his collar bone, before she pecked him on the cheek and left.

"Phone her about what?" Alys asked sulkily as the door shut behind the presenter.

Owen smiled at her.

It wasn't funny. He was enjoying that she was jealous. What right had Julia, to come in here, swanning around? Making him happy again.

"Alys, come here."

His mood had definitely lightened. Little by little with the help of Rhys, and annoyingly Julia, he was emerging from his blackest days of depression.

She sloped towards him and perched at the edge of the sofa.

Trying to move her closer to him, his arm flailed as he failed to reach her without moving his elevated leg.

She finally obliged, shimmying over.

Putting his arm around her, he drew her to his chest.

"I'm sorry," he whispered into her damp hair. "I've been in a bad place. I've been a self-absorbed bastard to live with."

She sniffed, a little overcome.

"You've had a massive setback. Life-changing."

"Yeah, but things'll be okay from now on. They've offered me a job."

"A job?"

"Julia put me forward. They've offered me a seat in the pundit box. It'll only be for the final couple of matches this season, and then they'll review it. So no guarantees. But Julia says the coverage of my break means I'm hot."

Alys screwed her nose up.

"She thinks you're hot. You don't need to tell me that."

Owen pinched her nose.

"No. As in, people want to watch me on TV. They've all seen my break. It was so gory, it went viral. Apparently, it's had five million hits."

His eyes were lively, dancing again as he spoke. He was coming back to her.

The only thing that still niggled her, was why Julia Johnson, television star, had come all the way to Cardiff to give Owen a career break? Was the phone signal in London that bad? Did they not have producers who did that kind of stuff?

"Well, what d'you think?"

"Will it make you happy?"

"Yes."

"Then, go for it."

His eyes slipped over her seductively.

"What did I do to deserve you?"

He kissed her deeply and began lifting her sweatshirt.

"I love you, Alys. I want you with me. Back in my bed every night."

She sighed. At last. She'd been waiting for those words, these moves, again. She'd been right all along. What she had with Owen was different to Leo.

"Hold on, I've got something for you."

He gave her a mock-pained look as she readjusted her sweatshirt and went to get the velvet pouch from her bag. It wouldn't harm him to make him wait a little longer.

"I've been meaning to give you this back. It's supposed to protect warriors." She shrugged. "A bit late for that now."

He slipped the signet ring on. It fitted perfectly.

"I'll always wear it."

He pulled her back to him.

"Now, where were we?"

"Owen, you're injured."

"My leg is. But that doesn't mean we can't, ya know, get a bit creative."

She grinned at him. He was very creative.

Breathing a huge sigh of relief, she began to take off her jumper.

His hand held her arm in place. It was him that was stopping her from undressing, this time.

"Alys? That new underwear you bought? The sexy black outfit."

"What? The basque?"

"Yeah, that. Go put it on."

"Do you want to see the other things as well?"

"Other things?"

"Yeah, I've got a couple of surprises. Toys you might be interested in."

Owen's eyes darkened.

"I thought I was in control in the bedroom?"

She ran her teeth over her bottom lip. Dare she do it?

"Not while you're injured."

He cocked his head at her.

"Is that right?"

She steeled herself.

"Absolutely. As long as you can't move. As I see it, you're my captive."

She grabbed the curtain sash behind her and surprised him by tying it tightly over his eyes.

"Complain and your hands'll be cuffed as well."

"What? Proper handcuffs?"

Owen bristled. His vision now gone.

She whispered close to his face, "Yes, with only one key that I will keep. How does it feel, not being in control?"

"*Ahh!*"

Her hand brushed over the hardening lump in his shorts. Then, squeezed hard.

He blew out a deep breath.

He felt her shift away from him and his head strained in search of her, trying to find her lips. But she'd ducked out of his way.

"No. You're gonna do exactly what I want now. And quite frankly, Owen Morgan, I've been waiting for you long enough."

She put her lips to his good ear, her hot breath tantalising him as she trailed her tongue and lips over his neck, then back up to his ear. Biting his lobe. Surprising him again.

He groaned.

"Today, Owen, you're gonna fuck me hard. Again and again. But only when I say. You got that?"

"Oh God, Alys! Go get that basque on. Now."

"No, Owen. You're gonna wait there until I'm good and ready to wear it."

"Alys. Come on. What do I have to do here? Beg?"

"Yes. You do. And you will be. Believe me... While I'm gone, you better think up a safe word. I will be back, 'cos if you're a good boy, I'm going to be dedicating myself to your pleasure all afternoon."

His lips curled below the curtain tie.

"And if I'm bad?"

"Then... you'll be punished," she whispered, twisting his nipple through his t-shirt, making him breathe hard. He was fired up. He'd take her now if he could. But she'd gone.

Owen sank back into the sofa as he waited for the sound of Alys' voice. Hopefully, she'd be back with him real soon in that sexy black number.

He could feel his heart thumping as he listened out for her.

Was that the fridge? If he was lucky, there'd be whipped cream, and what about some of her chocolate mousse? He'd definitely be down for that.

He honestly had no idea what she was going to do next. Pain? Pleasure? A bit of both. He was as horny as hell.

He'd always been the playmaker. Cuffed. Blindfolded. He was in new territory here. At her mercy, for once. And who'd have figured it was such a turn on?

He loved that she was adventurous. They were so compatible. His life was changing. New things were scary. Out of his control. Like this. He was going to have a hard time learning to let go.

But with Alys with him, it promised to be one hell of a ride.

CHAPTER 20

--------*--------

I t felt surreal. Alys was watching the rugby match in her room in The Lobster Pot and there was Owen, on the television discussing the key play and tactics of the rugby game.

It was near the end of the season now and Owen had been given two match commentaries as a trial. This one was in Cardiff, and there was one in Twickenham a fortnight later, where he'd be commentating on England's final game of the season. If he did well, the producer said he'd get a regular pundit role for September's World Cup in Argentina. He wouldn't be out there, it'd be done from a studio in London with a green screen.

Owen was dressed in the smart shirt and trousers she'd bought him earlier that week. It'd been a mission to find trousers wide enough to cover his booted lower leg without him looking like John Travolta in Saturday Night Fever.

On screen, he came over as relaxed, talking knowledgeably and wittily. And very photogenic. Not only did he look hot, in Alys' humble opinion, he was totally at ease with the cameras. He was talking as if he was on the sofa in someone's living room, not in front of millions of viewers.

Feeling a sharp pang, she saw his signet ring and realised how much she was missing him. She touched the swan around her neck.

The camera cut to pitch-side and there was Julia Johnson, looking glamorous in a long wool coat and a cute scarf. Large microphone in hand, she was interviewing the man of the match. Flirting, more like.

It was getting more and more difficult to get time to see Owen now she'd gone back to work. And with April around the corner, Beth needed Alys in Freshwater Bay. Baby number two would be making its entrance any time soon and The Lobster Pot was getting busier with tourists now that spring was here.

Alys did her best to see Owen, getting the train to Cardiff on her days off. And when she was there, their relationship was as strong as ever. Things were sweet between them again. He still had to rest the leg and he was hobbling about on crutches, but simply spending time together was enough for both of them.

The programme finished and Alys got ready for her evening shift. She was leading service tonight because Paul had organised a fundraiser in the bar.

He was holding a promise auction to raise money for prosthetic limbs for the child amputees in Laos. The trip with Vanessa had fired something inside Paul and he'd spent time when he was out there visiting villages with a charity and learning about the devastating effect unexploded devices still had on the villagers, particularly the children.

And Beth wasn't slowing down, either. Even in her last month of pregnancy, she was flat out getting La Galloise ready. They were aiming for a summer launch.

The design of La Galloise was modern. Gone was the traditional French bistro, it was now wall to wall glass, strong teal tones and elaborately patterned tiles. Ariana had been the creative director behind the decor and had given the place an almost colonial French feel to it. Moroccan even.

Alys loved it. It made the modern space intimate, even with all the big windows and views.

The bar below the restaurant was all out beach shack, with lots of corrugated sheeting and surfboards. Once they'd got that going, Alys knew the shabby Lobster Pot's days were numbered.

"Did you see me?"

Owen was on the video call, his face animated.

"Yes, you were fantastic."

"Was the mark-up over the video too much?"

"No, it was perfect. Did you enjoy it?"

"Yeah, I did. I hope they keep me. It depends on viewer feedback. It's great still being involved in it all."

Owen, darling, we're all heading out. Post-show drinks. You coming?

Alys picked up the familiar voice in the background.

"You off out, then?"

"Looks like it. I miss you, Alys. I wish you were here with me."

"Me too. Enjoy yourself. You were fab today."

The call ended, leaving Alys feeling flat. It was irrational, but she couldn't help it.

She couldn't put her finger on it, but Julia Johnson unsettled her. Whatever happened, she needed to make sure that she got over to Cardiff on her next days off.

"That was fun."

Vanessa slouched into the sofa and rubbed her eyes.

Paul placed the mugs of tea down on the table and joined her, sitting close beside her, both of them exhausted from the busy promise auction.

"Eighteen hundred pounds. That's phenomenal."

He sank back into the sofa.

"Yeah. We'll wire the money to the charity, and next time we go out we can record the stories of the children we've helped."

Paul was proud. He hadn't done anything like this since he was in the paras, and here he was making a difference again. If it hadn't been for Vanessa he'd never have ventured into anything like this.

"V?" he broached. He'd been mulling it over for a while. "D'ya wanna move in with me?"

Vanessa stared at him blankly.

"What's wrong with what we have, Paul?"

"Nothing. I thought that it'd be easier all round if you moved in with me and Sam. I don't like thinking of you all alone out here, up this quiet lane."

"Paul, it's *my* place. I happen to like living on my own with the birds, the rabbits and the badgers."

"Okay."

He thought she'd be pleased.

"I'm not simply gonna give up everything I've built to go shack up with you. And, why have I gotta move?" she carried on, ranting by now.

He was sorry he ever mentioned it.

"Look, it was only an idea. If I'd 'a known you'd get all pissy 'bout it I'd never of... I thought it'd be safer for you, that's all."

"*Safer?*"

"Yeah. After your truck was keyed."

"That happened in town. *I don't believe this!* You're doing what Lee used to do. Messin' with my head. Making me feel unsafe."

"What? No! I didn't mean anything by..."

"D'ya not get it?"

She was shouting now.

"You're overreacting."

"I'm overreacting? I'll show you overreacting. *Get out!*"

"What?"

"Go on. Leave."

Paul was gawping at her in disbelief.

"Is that what you want?"

She dug her heels in.

He stood up and grabbed his jacket off the chair.

"Yes. *Go.*"

Paul's jaw set firm.

"Okay, I will."

"Good."

"Good. And don't bother calling me, 'cos I won't answer."

"Suits me, 'cos I won't call."

The door slammed and Paul left.

Leaving Vanessa alone.

Gaslighting is what the women at the shelter called it. It was like losing her mind. Was Paul doing it too? Making her feel un-safe, so he could play the great protector. The super-hero sol-dier, who'd lock her away and keep her as his.

Lee had said he was protecting her from herself. Her head hadn't been clear. He could have been drugging her. It wouldn't surprise her. Not much did about Lee.

She'd still be there now if it hadn't been for her friend, Natalya who'd helped her make contact with the women's shelter and facilitated her escape one night after work. Giving herself to Lee, Natalya gave Vanessa the chance to escape through a side door. To find the car that was waiting for her to take her to the shelter.

She'd never forget the kindness of the other women at the club. They had a whip-round after. Five hundred for her. Five hundred for Natalya to get her teeth fixed when she got out of the hos-pital.

Lee was banged to rights for grievous bodily harm and dealing in drugs. And Vanessa moved as far away from London as she could. The place under the ruler on the map had said 'Holy-guard'. She liked that name. It sounded like God was protecting her. A fortnight later, a worker from the shelter put her onto a train at Paddington Station.

And here she was again. Another man. This time, a good one. But, even so, like all the men in her life, he couldn't help himself. He had to control her.

Alys didn't sleep a wink. She'd been itching to call Owen all night, but had thankfully resisted. It'd be like she was trying to catch him out. She had to trust him.

He'd rejected Julia before, she told herself, repeatedly. Yes... but, the doubt in her head needled her. But, she'd been there, then. In his apartment. He'd come to her bed, after.

Julia was still trying to hunt Owen down, to steal him from her. Would he be tempted? Julia was so smooth and polished, compared to her. At least two dress sizes smaller. Plus, Owen owed her now.

After hours of sleepless agonising, early the next morning she tried his phone. How would she react if it went onto voicemail?

It rang. And relief washed over her as he picked up straight away. He was in his sports gear, looking fresh.

"Hey, Alys. You caught me doing a few upper body weights."

He paused.

"You look exhausted."

"I'm fine. Did you have a good night?"

"Not too bad. I missed you, though. When can you come over again?"

She rubbed her face. She was losing the plot. She hated being apart from him.

"I'm off Wednesday and Thursday this week?" she suggested.

"Oh, I can't do then. I've gotta go to London."

"London? How you gonna get about with your leg?"

"They're sending a car."

"To Cardiff?"

"I know. Mad, eh? There's an agent interested in me and they wanna discuss other opportunities."

"Like what?"

"Sports quiz shows, celebrity appearances. Stuff like that."

Alys laughed.

"I can help you with any baking competitions."

"And there's a month in the Australian bush in December, apparently."

Alys giggled.

"If you want a bush tucker trial, I can cook you crocodile steaks."

"Is that what they do?"

"Pretty much. They make you eat witchetty grubs, fisheyes and kangaroo willies."

He pulled a face.

"Seriously? I'm not doing that."

She turned her gaze at the swan he was wearing around his neck. He never took it off, except when he'd been playing rugby.

"Sounds like things are taking off for you."

"Yeah, Julia's interviewing me on her show, Wednesday night." She shivered.

"Alys? What's up?"

"You're getting very close to Julia again."

His face clouded over.

"What you trying to say?"

"Nothing. I love you, Owen. I miss you, that's all."

"I miss you too, Alys."

CHAPTER 21

--------- * ---------

P aul had been miserable all week. Vanessa had told him in no uncertain terms that it was over. She wasn't prepared to change a single aspect of her life for him. And Paul had Sam, and even Dan, to consider. He couldn't desert them and bunk up with Vanessa. And anyway, being practical, her place was too small for them all.

He was offended that she'd compared him to her ex-husband. That was nuts. He'd been concerned about her safety, that was all. He'd been trying to look after her. That bastard had mentally scarred her.

Still, however he squared it, there wasn't a future for them. Not while she was so bloody-minded. Good thing that she was flat out on the marquees. They were doing six or seven weddings a week through the spring and summer. Neither of them had the headspace to sort this out.

Sitting in the kitchen after service together, Paul poured his heart out to Alys.

"Sometimes you drift apart," he told her sadly.

Alys sighed.

"But, surely, you still love her?"

"Yeah, 'course I do. But, when you both want different things and you're moving in different directions... Love alone. It's not enough."

❖ ❖ ❖

Paul's words stuck like an earworm as she lay in bed, alone. After the late shift, she'd streamed Julia's show. The woman was shamelessly flirting with Owen in front of millions of viewers. It was cringe-worthy.

From Owen's body language on screen, he was on his guard with her too. His face was all smiles, but she could tell he was keeping his distance from Julia. He was polite back. Never flirtatious. There was no reason at all not to trust him. She should be relieved.

But, putting Julia to one side, Owen was heading for a huge television career, probably in London. She hardly saw him as it was these days. How was their relationship going to last when he was a celebrity star, skating with the stars, baking cakes and jumping out of a plane with a bunch of celebrities in the Aussie jungle?

God, how she longed for him to be with her now. Still aching for him, she drifted into a restless sleep until her phone went off, waking her up with a start.

Alys groaned. It was pitch black. Two-thirty. What was going on? Was it Owen?

She swiped the phone to answer the call.

"Oh, gosh!... I'll be there now."

The baby was on its way and Alys had agreed to be on standby to look after Finn.

Shaking herself fully awake, she grabbed the head torch and the backpack she had at the ready and left The Lobster Pot, jogging up the hill past La Galloise and down towards the boathouse.

Owen's boathouse, she reminded herself. Though he wouldn't have the place until Gareth had finished their new family home.

Beth was getting into the car when she arrived.

"Don't worry about Finn," Alys told them.

Gareth nodded and started up the pickup. Beth's contractions were coming regularly and the hospital was a fair drive away.

She settled down to sleep on the sofa downstairs, ready for when Finn woke up. She hoped that Beth's labour would be smooth.

Baby number two. Who'd have thought it? A couple of years ago, Beth had worried that she'd never be able to have kids.

Babies had never been on Alys' agenda. And judging by the way she sensed things were heading with Owen, she wasn't sure if they'd be happening any time soon.

Vanessa rubbed her temples as she listened to the upset caller, the phone against her ear. Understandably, the mother of the bride was beside herself. It was Thursday morning and the marquee had gone up yesterday in a field beside a Celtic stone circle. Ready for the Friday wedding.

And now it was all ruined.

When the bride's mum had got there with her friends, ready to decorate the inside of the marquee, they'd found massive knife slashes through three sides of the canvas.

When she got there to assess the damage, her worst fears were confirmed. It was far too bad to patch. The marquee was completely ruined.

Vanessa checked. She had one spare marquee in store. It was bigger and had side windows along it. But, it would have to do.

She calmed everyone down and put in some calls, organising the replacement and quickly amassing a gang to refit the marquee. She sent the mother of the bride off for a coffee with her friends. Everything would be sorted by lunchtime, she'd assured her.

She started taking photos of the damage with her phone. Another police report. Another insurance claim.

Who would do such a thing? Perhaps there was an angry ex, seeking revenge?

The important thing was that they'd get it fixed, and tomorrow everything would be perfect and the guests would never know.

She made a mental note to talk to the mother of the bride about security. She had a contact, a firm who would come check on the marquee regularly overnight. Make sure nothing else happened in the next twenty-four hours.

It was most likely to have been kids up to mischief. Mindless vandalism.

Or? It struck her like a lightning bolt.

It was Paul. He was trying to make her afraid. Trying to take her independence away.

Paul was surprised when he spotted Vanessa moving across the Lobster Pot car park like a twister in the Kansas dust.

There was nothing much more for either of them to say, but judging from the way she was barrelling towards the pub, it looked like she still had plenty. What the heck had he done now?

Anticipating trouble, not wanting an audience, he went into the lounge bar to head her off. It was too late.

"If you wanted to speak with me, you only needed to call me," she launched at him as the door swung open.

"What?"

Paul stared at her, dumbfounded.

"That marquee cost me over a grand. And it's completely wrecked."

"Vanessa, what are you talking about?"

"Don't play dumb. You know what."

"I don't. Honest. I'm lost."

"I'm calling the police."

"Sounds like a good idea. We can do it from here. Vanessa, please tell me what's happened?"

"That's what *he* used to do. Act all innocent. Like butter wouldn't melt."

He raised his hands up, exasperated.

"What's going on? Tell me."

Slumping onto a barstool, she slouched forward and broke down. Her head in her hands on the bar.

A couple of locals pretended to look at their drinks or glance away. The whole village would be gossiping about this later.

"V, let's go in the back."

She glanced up at him, eyes reddened, mascara smudged.

Putting his arm around her back, he led her through the kitchen door and sat her down by the stainless-steel prep table.

He left to make her a cup of tea and get some tissues.

There was one junior chef left, cleaning out the large saucepans in the sink.

They were as alone as they could be.

He took the tea and tissues through to her. He could do with something stronger. He liked things simple. He didn't need this kind of drama in his life.

Pulling up a stool, he sat beside her.

"Vanessa. Please believe me when I say I have no idea what it is that's upset you. I still love you."

She looked at him in disbelief.

"Yes, call me nuts, but I still do. And if I can help you, I will."

She looked at him unsteadily, unsure of which part of that speech to tackle first.

Wiping her cheeks with the back of her hand, she swept her hair off her wet face. Then, using the tissue paper she mopped her eyes and blew her nose.

"My marquee's been slashed."

She got out her phone and showed him the pictures.

"I'm sorry I lost it, back there. I thought you'd done it."

Paul was horrified. What was going on in that head of hers? It was beyond complicated.

It had been quite a day. Alys covered the last part of the shift, to help Paul get over to Vanessa's early. Gareth was back from the hospital and looking after Finn. This morning, Beth had given birth to another baby boy. They'd named him Evan, after Gareth's uncle who'd left them the original restaurant. He was the reason they'd met each other.

Alys was pleased. She'd adored their Uncle Evan too. And it was a fitting tribute to the wily Welsh chef who'd been a regular at La Vie en Rose, the London restaurant where Beth and Alys had worked together as chefs.

Paul had a bottle of wine in his hand as he rang Vanessa's doorbell. The way she'd reacted to him this afternoon, they had to talk about it. He'd had plenty of rows with women in his time, but nothing like this. Vanessa was certainly a test. Dangerous even. He was still reeling from her wild allegations.

Suddenly, he had cold feet. Turning up on her doorstep like this, out of the blue, it could be misconstrued. She could twist his intentions. Accuse him of stalking her? He turned to go.

"Paul?"

He was halfway back down the driveway.

"Sorry. I didn't want to disturb you. I came to give you this. Cheer you up... Uh, I won't disturb you. I better go."

He held the bottle out in front of him but made no move to walk towards her.

"Paul."

She stood on the doorstep. A stand-off.

"I'm sorry about today... Don't go."

Her voice cracked. And a little piece of his heart melted.

He sighed and followed her inside the house.

They sat at the kitchen island. A couple of glasses and the bottle opener. Wine as yet unopened in front of them.

"You must think I'm loopy."

He regarded her warily.

"No. But, it's not usual, Vanessa."

She studied her fingernails, her forehead crinkled into a frown.

"Ever heard of gaslighting?"

Paul stared at her blankly.

"Look it up. It's what some men do to control women. It's like a drip-feed of doubts, insecurities and lies."

"Lee?"

She fixed her gaze on him.

"It makes you begin to doubt yourself. Not believe anything anyone says. After a while, you lose your mind... I'm still a mess."

There was treading on eggshells, but this was reaching a whole new level. How was he going to cope with everything he said being deconstructed; misconstrued?

"Vanessa, I'm a simple guy."

She sighed, but he carried on.

"I'm not that smart. I barely got through high school."

Her lips curled as both of his hands reached out and took hers. He held onto them loosely.

"If I say something you don't like the sound of, why don't you call it as you see it? So, we can then go through all the angles and check you're happy. Would that work for you?"

She considered that for a moment.

"Yeah, we could try."

"If you can't say it, 'cos it's too painful, then write it down. But we've gotta talk it all through calmly. Not get angry with each other or worry about the reasons why we're doing something."

It was his last shot. If this didn't work, he'd have to walk away.

"Paul?"

Her eyes found his.

"I trust you."

CHAPTER 22

---------*---------

O wen sat on a shiny black leather sofa in the reception area of a large windowed office on the fifteenth floor of the London office block.

He'd been in London for three days this week, which meant he'd not seen Alys again. He missed her. It had been over three weeks since they were together last. And even though they talked every day, he longed to wrap his arms around her and feel her up close against him again. Feel her lips on him. Feel himself inside her.

The Julia situation was painful. She'd been chasing him relentlessly and he was starting to feel harassed. Initially, she'd been useful, teeing him up with the rugby job and getting him the agent contact after he'd appeared on her show.

But then, she'd propositioned him relentlessly over dinner. He hadn't wanted to go, but after she'd interviewed him on her show she'd insisted on going for food. She'd spent all night flirting with him, moving her foot up his good leg under the table, she even tried to rub her hand up his thigh.

He'd moved it off him and told her to stop it. She told him to go to Hell. She was losing her dignity. He wanted as little to do with her as possible. But, she was difficult to avoid. They swam in the same pond.

"Mr Morgan? Stephanie's free now."

Stephanie's P.A. guided him through to the sumptuous office.

Full-length windows with a London river view. Expensive art on the walls. Stephanie was the most prestigious agent in the business, with a bevy of sport star celebrities on her books. Their framed heads stared at him from one wall. A rogue's gallery of sports star headshots, with space for one more. Would his head be placed like a trophy alongside them?

A middle-aged lady with thick red-rimmed glasses and a grey bob, there was an air of creativity about her, cut in with a hard nose for business. She wore a shapeless grey linen dress with two thin sticks of black-stockinged legs sticking out from the hem.

Stephanie shook hands warmly with him as he came in and then retreated back behind her desk.

She paid minute attention to every detail. Apprising him as he sat down opposite her. It felt like a job interview.

"Ahh, Owen, pleased to meet you at last. How's the leg?"

"Coming out of the boot in a few weeks. Then it's more physio, and we'll see… I still get some pain. My rugby playing days are over."

He could say that out loud now, though it was still hard to accept.

"And…?"

She scanned through the resume in front of her, and raised an eyebrow.

"You're a doctor I see?"

"Not medical. Psychology."

She cocked her head, evaluating him for the longest time. Owen sat still, holding her gaze. Seeing it as a battle, refusing to be out-powered by her. His hand absently stroked his signet ring.

"Interesting."

Her attention drifted to another document from the file.

"Initial feedback from our focus groups has been very positive. The video of your ghastly injury means you're very recognisable with the younger demographic. All those hits on YouTube, that's impressive."

"I didn't try."

She peered at him over her glasses.

"Hmm. Quite." She carried on reading. "Your voice is playing well too. For some reason, audiences like rich Welsh accents. Trustworthy, apparently. Great potential for adverts."

She eyed him levelly.

"And you'll be pleased to know that your sex appeal factor is high. The report says that you've got the yummy mummy vote."

For the first time, Owen squirmed.

"My life is complete."

"Comedian. I'll make a note."

He felt like he was in the headteacher's office.

"We can swing some primetime stuff. Sports quizzes, of course. General Knowledge quizzes and daytime panels, everyone gets those. And I may be able to tee you up for Baking with the Stars."

"Great."

"You're a little too old for celebrity love programmes," she said assessing him carefully. "Although I'm sure you'd spruce up very well in fake tan and Speedos."

"I dunno if I wanna do..."

Leg'll be healed by September?" she cut across.

"Hope so."

"Hmm... Better steer clear of ice-skating and the ski-jump shows for this year. I'll have a word with the producers, see what I can do about getting you dancing next year."

Owen tried to comprehend everything she'd said. This was not what he'd been expecting at all. What had he been expecting?

"Can you give me some time?"

She stared down her glasses at the six-five man in front of her.

"Things move fast around here, Owen. You've got two weeks and then we'll be moving on. This is the industry of the Hot and Not. And Hot doesn't last long. *Believe me, honey.*"

"Are you sure that Beth can spare Alys for three days?" Owen asked Paul over the phone. "I'll pay for any extra cover. Agency staff. Whatever. I have to see her."

It had been a week since Evan Morgan had made his first cries in the world and mother and baby were doing well. Finn, on the other hand, was not so good. He'd thrown a couple of tantrums and Gareth had been run ragged. Neither Gareth nor Beth was getting much sleep.

When he'd called his brother, he'd said the same as Paul. If it was something that he absolutely had to do, then they could spare Alys. But, not for long, they were on full stretch.

In the end, he begged three days and Paul pulled a few strings. An old friend was going to stay with him and cover Alys' shifts. Owen knew he was asking a lot. But he hadn't seen Alys for a month. And it was starting to feel like make or break.

He wanted to surprise her, so he was going all out on this one. He had a driver coming to collect her. He'd bought her the outfit and the shoes for her to wear, with help from Ariana. And he was going to whisk her away to the awards party that he'd been invited to at the Grosvenor in London.

He had other surprises too for her. But he'd see how things played out first. He wanted her advice about Stephanie's offer, and he couldn't discuss it with her over the phone.

How would she feel about moving to London? She'd lived there before, and it was where the best restaurants were. The appearance fees as a celebrity on these programmes were huge. They'd never need to worry about money again. Not that he did now, after his long professional sports career. But she'd never have to work again either, if she didn't want to.

He was still wrestling with it all. He'd never thought of himself as a celebrity. He could generally walk the streets of London without too much recognition.

Wales was a different matter because everyone was genuinely rugby crazy. The photo with Britney from Barry had been a wakeup call.

How dare he!

He hadn't even asked her. When Paul told Alys that Owen had booked her three days off, she was bouncing. And the last thing Beth needed was a stranger covering so she could go off on a jolly. Especially considering she'd taken over a month out to help Owen after his injury.

But, in spite of all her misgivings and her bitching, she'd still booked herself into a beautician in Holyguard for a little surprise for him. And she still got into the big black Mercedes that pulled up outside the Lobster Pot Inn at six the next morning.

When the car arrived at his apartments, Owen met them at the entrance. He was now moving with a single crutch and a support boot had replaced the gruesome frame. The specialists were pleased with how the bone had healed, although he still had to take extra care and wasn't allowed to walk far.

He slid into the back of the car beside Alys. The brush she gave him on the lips felt cold.

"You alright?"

"I'm fine. Just tired. Early start."

They began battling through the Cardiff rush hour traffic towards the motorway. There was a long spell of silence.

"How's life with the A-Listers?"

"One long party. How's life at the Lobster Pot?"

"The same. Apparently, the owner's a total plonker, but the staff are great."

Her lips curled sarcastically and she turned her head, staring out of the window.

"Alys, you're mad at me."

"I'm not."

"Don't lie. I've got that cereal packet degree, remember."

She threw him a look.

"You've no idea how busy and how short staffed we are. And you never asked me. You went behind my back. Paul's called in favours and he's covering for me on his days off, which isn't fair. You only thought about yourself. And you just presumed I'd come."

He tried to take it in, but it was early. Maybe, she needed coffee?

"I'm sorry Alys. But, it's been a month. If I hadn't done this, I'd never have seen you."

"Oh, that's rich. On my days off you're always in bloody London."

They sat in moody silence as the car smoothly made its way over the bridge and into England.

"Sorry. I should have asked you first."

"Yes, you should've."

She leaned her head on his shoulder and closed her eyes.

When she woke up, they were in the London traffic and a truce had fallen between them. Owen had his arm around her. And Alys, never one to hold a grudge for very long, relaxed into him as he held her close.

Owen took her hand, giving it a squeeze as they got out of the limo at the front of the five-star Mayfair hotel. She squeezed it back, then gasped as she stepped inside the sumptuous lobby.

"You sure this isn't above our budget?"

"Shush Alys. Relax. It's all paid for."

They checked in and took the elevator up to the room.

Alys seemed to have been slipping out of his fingers these past few weeks. And there was no way that he'd ever let that happen. She was the love of his life. He hoped she wouldn't be scared off when he asked her. He'd go anywhere to be with her. He couldn't live without her and he wanted her with him by his side forever. Not living away from him, like now.

In the hotel room, he took her hand and sat her down on the bed. He brushed his hand over the back of her neck, and under her silky hair.

"Let's start again, yeah?"

"I'd love to."

Alys looked relieved. Her flirty smile filled him with hope. He could turn this around.

Taking her in his arms, he kissed her. Pulling her down with him onto the crisp, tightly made king-sized bed.

Feeling his way over the contours of her body, he stroked her tenderly. Brushing her with soft caresses, slowly stripping her of her top and then her short skirt. Her tights and her boots.

She fumbled with his shirt buttons, finding his defined chest and letting her hands explore him too. Touching and remembering the shape of his hard, muscular body. She stripped him too as he worked on her bra, freeing her breasts, her panties...

"Fuck. Alys!"

"Surprise."

His fingers lingered over her soft waxed folds.

"I need my mouth on you. Now."

"Shh... patience, or I'll have to start punishing you again. Ahh!"

She gasped as she felt his warm breath on her.

Then he heard her moan as his tongue swirled, and his mouth got to work. Eating her, feasting relentlessly, finding that spot. She let out a cry as she came on his mouth.

There was no time for patience. Or for slow.

Flipping her over, he arched her up onto her knees and elbows in front of him. Massaging her breasts he took her. Hilt deep. Pumping hard. Relentlessly. Needing her. Owning her body. Claiming her as his own as he spilled into her. Alys was his. And always would be.

They collapsed together onto the pillows. A tear had escaped. It was rolling down her cheek.

"What's up, cariad?"

"Nothing... It's silly."

"Tell me."

Holding her close, he gently kissed her tears away.

"I thought I'd lost you."

His heart was bursting.

"Never. Alys, I'm never letting you go."

CHAPTER 23

----------*----------

Owen was going all out. Making her feel like a princess, as he said he'd do. It was only after she got back from her hair and makeup appointment in the hotel salon that she was allowed to open the zipped bag he'd been carrying with him.

She was stunned when she saw the dress he'd bought for her.

"You like it? Ariana picked it."

"That girl has taste."

She carefully took the dress out of the bag and held it up against her. It was a full-length dark-green shimmering dress, fitted and ruffled around the body with a halter neck and a slit up the side.

She let out a whoop as she opened the cardboard shoebox at the bottom of the dress bag.

"*Jimmy Choo!*"

She opened the box and gazed, spellbound. They were high delicate court shoes with a gold spiked heel and a moondust-like glitter shimmering across them.

"Cinderella shoes."

She slipped on the dress and examined herself in the mirror. It showed off her curves and its green material set off her styled long auburn tresses perfectly. She'd never dressed up like this before.

Owen was looking incredibly buff too in his well-cut dinner

jacket and black tie. He was like a movie star. She smirked. James Bond, but with a cauliflower ear.

He was staring at her.

"What?"

"Alys, you look incredible."

She was thrilled.

"There's one thing missing, though."

Alys turned back to the mirror to see what was wrong.

"You can't wear that."

He was motioning at her swan necklace.

"What if we do a swap for tonight?"

He stood behind her and kissed her neck as he carefully lifted off her swan and then put his hands gently around her, fixing a new necklace in its place. A large diamond pendant set in a curling wave.

"Ariana's new range," he mouthed on her neck.

"It's too much, Owen. The dress, the shoes. Now, this. I can't."

"Alys, this is how I feel about you. We'll talk later. It's time to go and meet everyone."

Owen took her by the hand and led her down to the luxurious reception area and then through to the sumptuous function rooms that lay beyond the lobby in this vast hotel.

They were handed flutes of champagne as they made their way into the gala dinner and sports awards ceremony.

Alys had been to events like this before when she lived in London. Not long after she'd arrived there, in fact. That time, though, it had been her dressed in black holding a tray. She never for a moment thought that one day she'd be the guest. And with such a gorgeous man on her arm.

Stunned by the glitz, the glamour and beauty of it all, they made their way across the crowded mezzanine floor. From the bar reception area, two huge sweeping staircases took the guests to the vast hall below. It was covered with over a hundred fully laid out large, round banqueting tables.

The stage in front had a backdrop littered with small lights set into it like stars. Above the great room, sat lines of huge crystal chandeliers that sparkled with the light. Alys thought it looked like the ballroom of the Titanic. It was certainly as grand as anything she could ever imagine.

Walking into the crowd, Owen's heart flipped between pride and possessiveness, his inner caveman rising as he sensed the male eyes around him falling on Alys. They were in a room with hundreds of alpha sports stars, like himself. There was no way they were getting near his gorgeous girl. He'd beat them off with his crutch, if they tried.

Alys seemed oblivious to it all. She held his hand anxiously as they squeezed through the crowd.

There were some faces he recognised. Footballers, racing drivers, track athletes, cricketers, jockeys, even the odd rugby player. All were here for the sports awards and to raise money for a charity to help disadvantaged children have access to sport.

A familiar middle-aged lady with a sharp grey bob caught his eye and signalled him over.

"Alys," he said softly, "Come and meet Stephanie."

"Owen, honey. I'm *so* glad you came."

She air-kissed in the vague direction of his cheeks.

He introduced Alys to her.

No air-kisses for her. Stephanie's focus was fixed firmly on Owen.

"Have you got anything to tell me?"

"I'll get back to you very soon. I promise."

The pleasantries dropped away, she eyed him hawkishly.

"By the end of the week, Owen, or we'll be moving on."

Shifting her attention she promptly moved on too, greeting someone behind them.

Alys pulled a face.

"What was that about?"

"She wants to be my agent. Apparently, I'm hot at the moment. Everyone knows me from the video of my leg break. And I got high marks on the Yummy Mummy score chart."

Alys giggled.

"You go near any yummy mummies, and you'll never score again with me."

"Point taken."

"Owen!"

A cry from behind made him wince. What did *she* want now?

"Owen. Lovely to see you, darling."

Julia rushed over to him, wedging herself between the two of them.

She planted a kiss on him like a claim, then turned to Alys.

Owen shifted back to her side and took her hand.

"Hi Julia."

Alys couldn't hold a grudge against her, she'd helped Owen get his pundit job. She'd plated a big part in helping him get out of that dark place he'd been in. But it still grated. There were no two ways about it. The woman was a bitch.

She was certainly eye-catching this evening, Alys had to give her that. Julia was wearing a tight red dress with what boobs she had squeezing out of the top.

She already had three male footballer friends loosely in tow, although they'd broken off into their own small group, losing interest in her after she'd fixed her attention on Owen.

Taking a sip of her champagne, she rounded on Alys.

"How's Freshwater Bay?"

"It's a lovely place to live."

Alys sipped her drink. Trying her best to be sociable.

"Yes, the back of the boonies can be quite pretty in the spring."

"Well, as they say, there's no place like home," Owen chipped in.

Alys tried to get on the front foot.

"I loved your programme the other night. The one with the rescue dogs."

"*Ugh!* One of the smelly mutts peed on the sofa after... So, what is it you do in Freshwater Bay, anyway?"

"I'm a chef."

"Oh. A cook?"

Alys was grinning and bearing it, but she could feel the colour rising in her cheeks.

"And you're looking very well on it, I must say," she added, scanning Alys up and down.

Alys took the barb. Was Julia implying that she was freeloading? Or, that she was fat?

Owen threw Julia a hard glare.

She heard him mumbling under his breath at her.

"Julia, play fair."

Holding onto Alys' hand, he started to edge them away but Julia wasn't having any of it. Instead, she made a big drama of her empty glass and pleaded for him to get her another champagne. Leaving Alys with her, alone.

"How long a drive is Freshwater Bay from London?"

"Four or five hours."

"That's quite a drive. And even longer on the train, I should think?"

"Probably."

He sensed Alys' relief as Owen came back. He handed Julia a fresh glass.

"I wonder how you'll cope then when Owen moves here?"

"Julia."

Her eyes widened in mock surprise.

"It's only what you told me when we had dinner last week, darling."

Alys squirmed uncomfortably, her eyes hardening.

"Oopsy. Have I put my foot in it?"

Owen's face became thunderous, but Julia carried on, regardless.

"Oh! You've not told her everything, yet? Oh God! Me and my big mouth."

Alys was caught by the panic rising within her. Her eyes darted from Owen to Julia. Were they seeing each other, behind her back?

She needed to get some fresh air. She needed to breathe before she couldn't anymore.

How could he do that? Cheat on her, and then have that woman throw it in her face.

"Excuse me."

Picking up her dress, she turned and left them, dashing away through the throng of tall athletic men in dinner suits and the glamorous svelte women in designer dresses. Needing to get away from this place, barging a couple of people accidentally, trying to get through the crowd.

She faintly heard the voice of Owen behind her, calling her.

"Alys, wait."

He was trying to move through the crowd with his crutch, but people were in the way. And he was so big and the orthopaedic boot he was wearing was holding him back. By the time he'd got to the edge of the bar area, Alys was nowhere in sight.

Where had she gone? The place was huge.

Would she have gone back up to their room? Unlikely. He had the key.

She wasn't carrying her phone so he couldn't call her.

How dare Julia try and split them up like that? The woman was pure poison. But, he wasn't going to waste his time on the anger surging through him.

He had to find Alys.

It was then that he noticed her. She was sitting on a padded circular seat near the toilets, tucked out of sight. Her head was down, and she'd been crying.

He hobbled across the space and slumped down beside her.

"Alys"

"What the hell?"

The calm she'd borne throughout the exchange was gone. Owen saw the raw emotions in her face and it split him in two.

"Are you seeing Julia?"

"No!"

Owen put his hand under her chin, gently guiding her to look at him.

"She's bitter and twisted because I love you."

Alys' eyes stared at him doubtfully.

"And I've told her that."

He cupped her face in both of his hands.

"I promise you, I will never talk to that woman again."

Alys' lips tightened.

"You had dinner with her?"

"It was hardly that, Alys. We had food after her television pro-gramme. She's making it out to be more than it was."

Alys sniffed.

"You know what she's like. I told you about Paris. She did the same again. And yes, okay, she was all over me. But nothing happened. Believe me. It was embarrassing."

She scanned his eyes.

"Tonight, she was stirring things up," he continued. "It's what she does. The perfect Julia shitstorm. She can't accept that we're together."

"But, what about what she said? About you moving? To London?"

He leaned in and caressed her cheek gently.

"How would you feel about that?"

Alys wiped a tear off her cheek.

"I've lived here before. I'll go anywhere that you are, Owen. But I don't want us to be so long apart again. Honestly, I don't think our relationship will survive it."

He'd said he'd never let her go. He meant it.

He took her hand.

"Do you wanna get outta here?"

She nodded.

He stood up and pulled her to him, his arms caging her posses-sively.

"I'm starting to feel... a little suffocated by this place and we need to talk."

Her mouth curved weakly.

"Get changed and I'll take you somewhere."

"One of your secret special places?"

"Yes. But it's not like this."

They went back to the room and Alys called ahead.

Owen smiled when he saw her dressed in her jeans and those Jimmy Choos.

"The carriage may have turned back into a pumpkin but I'm still gonna wear these shoes."

Touching the small of her back he walked with her to the hotel elevator.

"Whatever you say, Cinderella."

CHAPTER 24

---------✹---------

They snuck out of the hotel like a couple of guilty teen-agers cutting class. Stephanie's agency had paid for their stay. But Owen was sure they wouldn't be missed.

They hailed a taxi and crossed the river, pulling up in the middle of a South London high street.

Taking him by the hand she led him up an empty side street to a paint-peeled door. A couple of industrial bins and a metal fire escape to one side, like a speak-easy there were no windows. Nothing from the outside would mark the place as a restaurant.

"You do trust me don't you?"

"Always."

"Well then, let me show you my favourite place in London."

Alys knocked on the door and the bouncer moved aside as she spoke the password she'd been given over the phone.

"This place is mad."

Owen chuckled as he stepped into a world he'd never have imagined lay behind the door. The restaurant ceiling was lined with huge coconut shelters, held in place by wooden poles wrapped in fairy lights.

Underneath, hurricane lamps and naked lightbulbs spread pools of soft light into the semi-darkness. The chairs and tables were painted bright turquoise, red and yellow and the bar was lined with coloured corrugated sheets. Large-framed vintage posters of dancers, music concerts and reggae stars covered the walls. It was a piece of the Caribbean in London. An homage to home.

The decor, shabby and homemade, was uber-chic. Authenticity, that's what it was, Owen decided. It didn't matter how hard the multi-national chains tried, they could never replicate this.

He beamed at Alys.

"What you been smokin' chef?"

He loved this place.

"You like spice, right?"

"Yeah?"

"Well, you've gotta try the jerk chicken. And, the sweet potato, coconut and pumpkin fritters are amazing. You've so gotta have some of those."

A reggae band was starting up on a raised stage area at the back of the restaurant, and Owen and Alys sat at a table near the bar, drinking rum punch as people casually drifted in for food and to listen to the music.

There would be plenty of dancing later. Although, it wouldn't be Owen.

"Take care with that," Alys warned him as he knocked his drink back like squash. "It's called punch for a reason. And they don't do measures here."

They switched to bottled beer as they shared the dishes in front of them. Goat curry with rice and peas. Ackee and salt-fish dumplings. The fritters Alys loved, and of course, the jerk chicken.

Owen took a swig of his Red Stripe beer. He cleared his throat, his eyes meeting hers.

"Alys, I've made up my mind."

"Yeah?"

This was so much better than any gala dinner.

"I'm not doing this anymore."

"*What?*"

His face filled with horror.

"*Oh God! No. Not us.*"

He'd genuinely scared her.

"What, then?" she said breathily.

"This celebrity thing. I've decided. I'm not doing it."

"I'm not following?"

"I know the money's amazing, right? But it's not for me. D'ya mind?"

"Mind what?"

"Mind me, coming home?"

Her face cracked. Reaching over the food, she kissed him, tasting the chilli in the jerk chicken he'd been eating. She ran her tongue over her burning lips.

"What? Coming home? To Freshwater Bay? That God-awful place at the back of the boonies?"

"Remind me will ya, Julia is banned from every pub in the village."

"It'd be my pleasure... I'll stick a picture of her on the dart board. Use her face as target practice."

She took one of the fritters.

"What made you decide?"

"I don't want to be around those people. I don't like them. But, last week too. I was sitting in Stephanie's office, and it struck me. I've trained relentlessly for ten years. Studying hard. Why am I signing my life away to make a complete pillock of myself tripping the Light Fandango on Saturday night primetime?"

Alys erupted into laughter.

"I'd love to see you in sparkly spandex."

Owen took a mouthful of the goat curry.

"Stephanie offered me a slot in the Celebrity jungle thing. I watched a clip. They were eating kangaroo penis."

"I'm sure your rugby mates would pay good money to see you sucking on cooked kangaroo."

"Don't go there, Alys," he warned, catching her infectious laughter, "I'm still recovering from your coq au vin."

"So, that's it. I've decided. I wanna be in The Lobster Pot."

"But, what about your psychology training?"

He started peeling the label on his beer bottle.

"What if we turned the Lobster Pot into a boutique hotel? Refurbish it so it's like a retreat. Somewhere to go to relax and focus on lifestyle and wellbeing."

"*Eh?*"

"Like fitness programmes. Cookery classes. Mindfulness and yoga. That kinda thing. Even one to one sessions for people trying to get their head around stuff. People could go there for therapy."

Alys caught the infectious sparkle in his eyes and he held her gaze.

"Somewhere like that would've helped me."

"It sounds awesome," she meditated. "Will it have a spa?"

Owen nodded.

"And a full gym, of course. But, I'll need help to do this."

She quirked a smirk and pointed at herself.

"What if we argue?"

"Then, we'll argue. I'm sure we'll sort it out. Of course, I'm always right, so you'll come 'round eventually."

"*Ha!* If you start getting all alpha on me, I'll get those cuffs out again. I enjoyed that."

He held her gaze.

"What if you were my equal partner in this?"

"What? Like business partner?"

Her eyes widened as he produced the box he'd been carrying around all evening from his pocket and opened it in front of her.

It matched her necklace. A platinum ring with a large diamond inlaid into a curved wave.

"Owen? What's that?"

"I love you, Alys. I want you with me forever. Will you marry me?"

Her face froze.

"You sure?"

"Yes, Alys. I'm sure."

He gave a nervous laugh.

"For God's sake, put me out of my misery. Please say yes."

"Oh, Owen, I love you so much. Yes. *Oh My God! Yes! Yes!*"

Leaning over the table, she kissed him full on the lips.

Owen gave a ragged sigh. For once that evening, one of his plans had worked out.

Soon, the whole restaurant heard they were getting married. The place became one big party, and by the time they crept into the hotel the gala dinner guests had long gone.

The evening hadn't been what Owen had planned. It had been so much better. In fact, he decided, it was the most memorable night of his life.

CHAPTER 25

---------*---------

Alys was examining her engagement ring, the only thing she was wearing as they lay in each other's arms late the next morning.

"Owen, d'ya still wanna get married?"

He nuzzled her ear and felt her quiver as they spooned together.

"You still want me, right?"

"Always."

She was so responsive. He was confident he could persuade her to do anything right now. He knew exactly which buttons she liked pressing.

He carried on working down her neck with his mouth.

"I bet when we tell them, everyone'll think I'm knocked up."

He stopped.

"You're not, are you?"

She punched him with her free arm.

"No! I don't want any buns in my oven. Not for a while yet, anyway. If it's alright with you? I want us to have time together first. Enjoy being a couple."

"Yeah, me too. I wanna live with you in that boathouse without having to make it toddler-proof."

"Couldn't we just do that?" she floated. "Live together. Weddings are so much fuss."

"I guess. The stag weekend'll be brutal knowing my rugby

mates,"

"You're gonna lose at least an eyebrow. Probably worse."

"Yip. I'll have to do it a couple of months before, so the photos aren't ruined."

He was on the same page as Alys. He couldn't be bothered with all that wedding drama.

"Where do we draw the line on who to invite? It could get huge."

He mentally tried to count and gave up.

"We'd have to have day and night guests. Then, there's the food, the venue, bands, bridesmaids and the hen dos," she listed.

He propped himself up on his elbow.

"More than one hen do?"

"Oh yeah. Weekend in Ibiza for the spring chickens and a spa day with the old chooks."

Even mentioning weddings made him feel exhausted.

"Is that what you want?"

She held up her left hand, rotating it so the diamond caught the light.

"No."

"Me either. It sounds hideous."

She pushed him flat and shimmied on top of him.

"I like what Gareth and Beth did, getting married in secret," she breathed into his ear.

"What would your mum and dad say?"

"Probably be relieved they're not footing the bill. They don't have much spare for fancy weddings."

"They'd never have to, Alys. Let's get married soon. A registry office. Real low key?"

"Hmm. Yes please. I've already got the dress," she added as he began pressing those buttons again. "And the shoes."

It was Paul who suggested coming over to Vanessa's house after work.

It was a bold suggestion and he'd rather have taken her out for a meal or gone away with her somewhere overnight, but he couldn't leave the Lobster Pot with Alys away and Beth at home with a new baby.

If he didn't see Vanessa, he was scared that things between them would slide again and it would all be over.

Judging by her warm reaction on seeing him and their passionate lovemaking afterwards, he was glad he'd been bold. Vanessa wanted them to get back on terms too.

He lay in bed in the darkness beside her mulling over everything that had happened between them. He wished he could move the relationship forward, but how could he when she was so fiercely independent and clear about keeping her own space?

If they tried, they could make living separately work. He'd have to get used to living out of an overnight bag. But was it what she wanted too?. It was going to take a lot of time and patience to get her to trust him unconditionally. He could do that, though. Vanessa was worth the wait.

He turned onto his side and was falling a slumber when the outside light flickered on.

He opened his eyes, and now fully awake, he lifted himself out of bed and moved silently to the window. He twitched the curtains to peep out.

There was nothing there. It must have been a fox or a badger crossing the yard.

Paul got back into bed and gently pulled the covers over him so he didn't wake her.

Suddenly, out of nowhere, the high pitched shrill of Vanessa's car alarm pierced the silence. The room flashed yellow as the SUV's indicators fired up.

Vanessa bolted awake.

Scrambling out of bed, Paul threw on his clothes and rushed to the front door, where the car keys were in the door lock.

He unlocked and opened the door, shutting it behind him. He scanned the driveway, there was no one about. Quickly, he aimed the keys at the SUV and de-activated the alarm.

It was a relief when everything fell silent again.

Holding the keys in his knuckles, he checked the vehicle. He couldn't see any obvious damage. Nothing appeared to be amiss. There were no windows open. No new scratches or dents. What caused the sensors to go off like that?

His military training kicked in. The air was still. The place was peaceful again. Yet, he sensed something. Like someone watching him.

He slowly scanned the garden, casting his eyes along the drive and then into the shadowy corners of the bushes and trees around the lawn. He wandered out towards the lane, looking searchingly into the fields beyond.

But it was a dark moonless night, and there was nothing much to see, except the shadows. And he caught no movements in the darkness.

Paul let out a deep breath. His eyes and his brain told him that this was purely a coincidence. A sudden gust of wind. Or an animal knocking against the SUV. Both were perfectly feasible. Perhaps. But, something else deeper, something primal, told him to be wary.

Of course, there was no way he could share his thoughts, without freaking her out. She'd only accuse him of scaring her so he could take charge.

But, Paul reasoned, this was the third thing to have happened to Vanessa. He was beginning to think there might be dots to join up.

Alys was desperate for Owen to meet Jo. Their friendship went way back. Back to when Beth and Alys both lived in London.

Jo was a journalist, an editor of an online news feed. She'd helped Beth out with La Galloise, getting it on the map as a foodie destination. And Alys was sure she could help them too with their plans for The Lobster Pot.

Alys filled him in on how Jo had been a key player in getting

Beth and Gareth back together. If it hadn't been for Jo's tenacity and her investigative journalism skills, Gareth would have lost Beth for ever. Jo had believed in them and their relationship, even when they'd doubted themselves.

When Alys had called her earlier that morning, Jo instantly re-arranged her diary so she could meet them for dinner. And there was only one place that Alys wanted to go.

Owen scanned his eyes over La Vie En Rose. It was very swanky. Slap bang in the City's financial quarter.

"So, this is where you worked with Beth?"

"Yes, and over there's table twelve. That's where your Uncle Evan sat every Friday at two o'clock."

"Wow."

It was odd to picture Uncle Evan sitting in the restaurant, friends with Beth and Alys long before any of his nephews knew them. Way before they'd ever heard of Freshwater Bay.

Uncle Evan had been dead a couple of years now, but Owen still remembered him fondly. Ellen said he got his strategic mind from his uncle. Judging by how Evan manoeuvred Beth and Gareth to meet and marry, he tended to agree.

Marcel, the owner of La Vie, greeted Alys with open arms as they came in. She spoke with him in fairly fluent French and he held her face proudly, then gave her another big French-style double kiss, shaking Owen's hand warmly when he saw Alys' engagement ring.

With Marcel guiding them to their table, they sat down.

"I must see the new restaurant once it's open. Tell Beth I'll be there, for sure. And I'll cook for you both. At your wedding," he told them. "Did you say Beth has *two* babies now?"

He produced a bottle of crisp white wine for them. It was all on the house, he insisted.

Alys waved and Owen turned around. At the door, a very confident, tall woman in a smart black trouser suit and a silver satin blouse scanned the room. She had a sharp black bob and bright cherry red lips. She carried a slim black briefcase bag.

She looked like she meant business. And she strode towards

them like she did too.

"On the booze already, Edwards."

She gave Alys a hug, then examined Owen as he stood up to greet her.

"Fucking hell, you're tall."

Owen raised an eyebrow as she promptly sat down and poured herself a large glass of wine.

"Blimey, Alys! You're engaged?"

Alys stuck out her hand so she could examine the ring.

Jo glanced up at Owen.

"First Beth. Now Alys. What is it with you Welsh men?"

"Come and see us, then you can find out for yourself."

"I'll be at the wedding, I hope."

Alys looked away.

"It's going to be family only," Owen responded.

"But you're coming, of course," Alys added hastily. She shrugged at Owen, and chewed her lip.

He wasn't sure what to make of Jo yet. But she was Alys and Beth's best friend, and she'd batted for his brother, got them back together when no one else could. That was good enough for him.

They ordered, and Alys filled Jo in on La Galloise and Beth's babies. It had been a while since Jo had seen her. They chatted through the meal and Jo told them about a big story she'd been working on. She called it modern-day slavery. It sounded pretty gruesome to Owen.

Jo had been tracking a Romanian gang, she told them. The gang tricked young Eastern European girls into leaving home, and trafficked them under false pretences to London. There, they were shipped out to cities and towns where they were kept as prostitutes in terrible conditions.

Alys shuddered.

"These guys sound dangerous."

"Ah, don't worry about me. I'm nearly there with it now. A few more weeks and I'll have the whole crime ring uncovered. I'm going to send the piece to a Sunday magazine as a freelancer."

Alys swirled the wine around in her glass.

"I liked it better when you were doing the Fashion and Cookery sections."

Owen floated his idea about the Lobster Pot. Jo was exactly the demographic he'd be aiming at. Stressed-out, workaholic alphas trying to re-find the balance in their lives.

"I think it's fabulous. Of course, you're the draw," she said staring directly at Owen.

"Eh?"

"Well, anyone can buy a big stately pile out in the sticks and put in a spa. What they're getting with you and Alys is the expertise. The fitness programme. The therapy. And the cookery school on healthy, clean food. Sell that and they'll all come. Guaranteed."

For all the ballsiness and bluster, Jo was incredibly sharp. And she was right. The Lobster Pot business model would succeed because of what they could offer it. Alys' protein recipes, his fitness programmes and the therapy sessions. He'd ask Vanessa too. Alys had gone to a couple of her yoga classes, and she taught mindfulness.

The Lobster Pot was beginning to take shape in his mind, and it made him even more determined to make a success of his plans.

CHAPTER 26

---------*---------

Back in Cardiff the next morning, Alys and Owen weren't for waiting. Today was the first day of their new chapter together. And Owen had no intention of spending a single night away from her. He was moving to Freshwater Bay.

They packed as much as they wanted out of his apartment, with Alys helping him to load it into his convertible. Owen reluctantly handed her the keys. With his foot in the boot, he still wasn't allowed to drive.

On their way home, they made a quick stop in Holyguard at the registry office where they noted their intention to marry and came out with a couple of dates. One was for early June.

Doable they decided, as long as they kept things small and Alys took the hint to keep a lid on the invites. But, Jo was different, she told him. She was like a sister to her.

After unloading Owen's things into the owner's apartment in the Lobster Pot, they bit the bullet. Alys drove them over to his parents' farm. Owen wanted to meet Alys' parents too, and ask her father formally. Alys cringed, but agreed.

It was a bright April day, full of sunshine and the promise of warmer times ahead. A good omen, Owen thought, as he got out of the car.

His fingers interlaced with Alys. And using a crutch in his other hand, he hobbled with her towards the lambing sheds where he'd spotted his mother.

"Well, well."

Ellen greeted them both as she put down the two empty milky wine bottles with rubber teats she was carrying.

"David, come here. Quick!" she shouted in Welsh.

"Why? What's up?"

Owen's father emerged from another shed where he'd been topping up the calf feeders.

Seeing his son with Alys and noticing the diamond ring on her left hand, he slapped his son on the back and gave Alys a kiss.

"Time for a cuppa?"

Over tea and plates of cake, Owen tactfully explained to his parents how they wanted a very small wedding, crossing his fingers under the table that his mother would not go off on one because the all cousins and extended family wouldn't be invited.

Thankfully, his mother agreed.

Rhys and Ariana's wedding had been bigger than either of them had planned, and it had been an awful lot of work. David and Ellen were off Down Under for three months and they'd already booked their flight tickets for June.

Owen checked the calendar on his phone and set the date with them all. They'd get married on the Saturday and his parents would be flying out Monday morning. He called the registry office to confirm.

Owen studied his mother as he held the line, waiting to be put through. She'd been uncharacteristically quiet. This wasn't about Alys. A nice Welsh girl, she liked her.

Something else was bugging her. And whatever beef she had, it was about to be aired. As he ended the call, his mother went on the attack.

"What's this I hear about the Lobster Pot? Why didn't you tell us? You didn't become a doctor to work a bar."

He sighed.

"I'm not a medical doctor, Mam."

She'd probably told the whole world he was a surgeon.

"It's a doctorate in psychology."

"That's the head, isn't it?"

"Well, yes, *but...*"

He gave up. It wasn't worth it.

Instead, he explained what they were going to do.

As he waited for their response, his dad was leaning back in his chair.

"As always, son, you've got it all mapped out."

Ellen was quiet again.

"I've still got the pundit gig on the television," Owen explained. "They've asked me to do the rugby world cup and the autumn international matches. The two careers will fit together well."

Alys chipped in, "Thankfully, he's turned down the opportunity to appear in celebrity dancing and game shows."

Owen winked at his mother.

"Rhys would never have forgiven me if I got to be more famous than him."

The next day, they took the long drive north to Alys' parents.

As she parked up in the street and switched off the ignition, she turned to Owen.

"This is going to be a bit of a shock for them. I've not mentioned you to them."

She took off her ring and stowed it in her pocket.

"I'll put it back on later, when you've asked Dad."

Owen didn't know what to make of that.

"Alys? Are you embarrassed about me?"

"No. Of course not." She sighed. "You'll see."

She pulled a face and quickly got out of the car, at the same time as the front door of her parents' terrace house flew open and Alys' mother rushed out onto the street.

She squawked as she hugged her daughter, then screeched as she saw Owen getting out of the sports car. She squealed again when she recognised who he was.

She hugged him. Kissed him. Felt his bicep as she called him 'a big lad'. Flapping around them, she ushered them off the street and into their small terraced house.

Her mother couldn't believe it. Alys had to take her through to the kitchen to calm her down.

Her daughter had snagged herself a famous rugby player. She was star-struck. She took more selfies with him than he'd ever had with Alys. She flirted outrageously. She even squeezed his bottom when she sat him down at the table for lunch.

She gabbled on non-stop as they ate. Alys' dad didn't say a word.

Owen suspected that the selfies would be all over social media by the end of the day. Then word would be out that they were engaged. It didn't bother him. But he hoped his friends wouldn't be too disappointed that they weren't coming to the wedding. Once the boot came off, he'd organise a night out with the boys.

But that would be after the wedding, and he'd insist that Alys stay over with him in Cardiff. It was more to protect himself, than anything else. Otherwise, knowing that lot, he'd end up bound in plastic wrap, naked and tied to a lamppost somewhere far away.

After lunch, Alys' father took Owen on a tour of his huge vegetable garden, which he called 'his office.' Between the raised beds, Owen asked him formally if he could marry Alys.

He came away with his daughter's hand in marriage and a dirty plastic bag full of new potatoes and Swiss chard.

"You can't get married without some form of hen party," Vanessa told Alys as they sat in the Lobster Pot lounge bar.

"We wanna keep things real quiet."

Vanessa had been spending more time with the girls. She got on well with the two chefs, and she'd been toying with the idea of asking Beth about branching out into wedding catering. Offering a whole wedding package could be lucrative.

Beth had snuck in with baby Evan on her way back to the boathouse to see how things were going. And she agreed wholeheartedly with Vanessa. Alys needed a girls' get-together before her big day.

Vanessa pushed on.

"Why don't the babies come along too? And we could have a couple of drinks and some tapas at mine? Just the girls."

"Sounds perfect," Alys agreed.

If someone had told her a month ago that she'd be a married woman by June, she'd have thought they were stark raving bonkers.

Vanessa was sorting out a small marquee for the wedding. It was going to be by the beach, at Gwen's cottage, where Rhys and Ariana were staying. True to his word, Marcel insisted on doing the catering and when she'd called Celine to tell her the news, she'd invited herself to the wedding too.

Owen had rolled his eyes when he heard. Alys couldn't say no. Apparently Celine was contacting Marcel. She'd put herself in charge of the desserts.

CHAPTER 27

---------*---------

He'd been watching her for over a month. The bitch. While he'd been locked up doing time, she'd been doing pretty well for herself.

He'd left her a message on that fancy truck of hers. The scratch was what he'd do to her face if she carried on seeing the prick that she was with. He saw him the other night at the house. Staying over. He'd sent them a little message then too. Waking them up with the car alarm.

He'd hidden in the bushes behind the house watching the tosser. She was scraping the barrel with him, alright. A middle-aged action man. Thought he was a tough guy, flexing his muscles as he came out of her door. Out of her bed.

Bet, she hadn't told him about the punters, and how she used to wrap her legs around that pole every night. Around the men, she'd done a lap dance for.

Dirty flirty Nessa. That's what she was. She always craved the attention. Could never get enough. And she always took the money they shoved into her knickers.

He did a three-point turn in the lane and parked the stolen hatchback in the passing place. He'd walk from there.

The car was ready for them to get away. Back to London where she'd be with him, again. Like before.

He felt the shortened metal barrel against him in the inside of his padded jacket. She'd better come without any bother. Get back to the old life. The punters and the pole.

He'd been watching her closely. She'd still got it. Though he could see too that he'd have to take a firm hand. Whip her back into shape again. Like the tiger, who'd thought it had gotten away, Vanessa would need to relearn the rules. Or have her teeth pulled out so she couldn't bite back.

Either way, live or die, she'd never be with that macho dick-head again.

"Wonder what they're doing now?"

Owen checked his phone, looking a bit bored.

There were some pool tables in the Lobster Pot's back bar. Paul was going to suggest a pool challenge. But, then Rhys had turned up with little Nansi asleep in the car seat by his side, and they couldn't very well leave her on the floor by the pool table.

Gareth had newly walked in through the door. Child-free.

"So, why no stag night?" he asked Owen, as he came to sit down with them.

Owen shot him a look.

"You know why."

Paul was confused.

"My mates are hardcore," Owen explained. "It'd be slammers, strippers and ritual humiliation. Anyway, neither Rhys nor Gareth had a stag night, as I recall."

That was true. Gareth got married in secret, and Rhys wasn't risking his sobriety.

Gareth rubbed his neck.

"Who was that rugby player they put in a mankini and got him shipped off in a lorry to Amsterdam?"

"What?"

"Johnny Jones," Owen answered. "His now ex-wife picked him up a week later from the Red-light District."

"What was he doing there for a week?"

"And which one got the pubic hair beard super-glued on him?"

Paul shook his head. He'd had his fair share of stuff like that in the army. He could understand Owen not being bothered with that anymore.

"The worst was the tattoo, though," Rhys reminded Owen.

"Ah yeah. That was too bad." Gareth agreed. "They inked the guy's ex-girlfriend's name onto his butt cheek. He thought he was getting a big heart with the date of their wedding on it."

Owen kept his face straight and stayed quiet. He'd been there, and he couldn't say categorically that it hadn't been one of his bright ideas.

"Nah. This suits me fine. If the boys rip me about it, I'll tell them I'm still injured. Too many pain meds to drink."

Vanessa put the plates of tapas on the coffee table. Beth had little Evan with her and Alys was rocking him as he drifted to sleep after his feed. Finn was staying overnight with Ellen and David.

"Thanks, Vanessa for hosting this, it's really kind of you."

Alys had gotten to know Vanessa better since she'd been doing more with Paul, and there was something about her that Alys liked. It was hard to describe. She had hidden depths.

"It's so nice to be out," Ariana yawned. "Wonder what the boys are up to?"

Vanessa looked at them. If she didn't spice things up, they'd all be flaked out, watching TV by nine.

"Right girls."

Vanessa had them all sat around the sofa and on cushions on the floor in the living room.

"What d'you all say we play a game?"

"Yey!" Alys cheered. "What kinda game?"

"A card game."

"Poker?" Beth asked.

"Not far off."

Vanessa smiled naughtily at her.

"Let's play the V-card game."

"V as in Vanessa?"

"Not quite, hun."

"No!"

Ariana had caught on before the others, and was going a little red.

She whispered what the game was about in Beth's ear.

Beth nudged her.

"Ah, come on, Ariana. It'll be a laugh."

Vanessa explained the rules of the game.

"You write down where you lost it, on the paper. Then fold it up and we have to guess who it belongs to."

They all agreed.

She passed the bits of paper round and they shared the pen as they wrote their secrets down and then popped the folded paper into a pot in the middle of the table.

"Okay, here goes."

She dramatically pulled out the first piece of paper.

"In a pub car park behind the bins."

"Ewww!" they all cried out, including the guilty party.

She pulled out another.

"At a festival in a muddy tent."

Everyone looked at each other, pulling faces. Any of them could have done that one.

"In a clown car packed up inside a lorry.".

"Ooh, Titanic with hooters," Beth giggled.

"And the last one. In an apartment looking out at the Eiffel Tower... *Ooh la la!* Very romantic."

As the bride-to-be, Alys got first guess.

"Uh... I'd say that Beth is the pub car park."

"What? I'm much more classy than that."

"Okay," Ariana screwed her nose up. "I think Beth's the muddy tent, then."

"Is that any classier?" Beth joked.

Vanessa called time on it.

"Beth, which one is it?"

"Neither. It was the Eiffel Tower view. I worked in France for a bit as a teenager."

"That one's the classiest," Ariana sighed.

"I was sure that was you," Alys said to her. "So, Ariana, which one were you?"

No one ventured a guess.

Ariana covered her hands in her face, peeping through her fingers.

"Pub car park," she winced as everyone looked at her in disbelief.

"What can I say? Not my finest five minutes."

She pointed at Vanessa.

"Clown car?"

"Ahh, yes. In the circus. Didn't do that again. The car doors collapsed and we both ended up bare-arsed on the floor."

"Alys, muddy tent?"

She nodded.

"Eisteddfod. It's a Welsh festival," she explained to Vanessa and Beth. "Teenagers let loose for a week, camping."

"Nansi is never doing that," Ariana sniffed. She'd been at them too.

They laughed and chatted until Rhys came to take Ariana and Beth home.

Vanessa refreshed their glasses of wine. Alys was in no rush to go. It was still early.

"What was it like growing up in the circus?"

"Relentless. Setting the tents up, practising acts, looking after the animals, promoting the shows. I never had any proper schooling. By the time I was fifteen, the circus was finishing. People didn't want to see the animal acts anymore. And I don't blame them, I always felt sorry for the poor things. We lived in a rented house for a bit, but I left home soon after and moved to London."

"Sounds tough."

"Yeah. It was. But now I look at my marquee business and I realise that working so hard back then gave me the drive to grow my business now, ya know."

Alice agreed.

Feeling a draught, Vanessa shifted and put her cardigan back on. "What was that?"

Alys glanced over her shoulder a little spooked.

"What?" Vanessa asked, taking a sip of wine.

"I thought I heard the door."

"Probably the wind."

"Nessa."

A man's gruff voice cut through the shadowy kitchen darkness. "Nessa, have you missed me?"

The cockney sounding voice growled again, sending a terrible shiver down Vanessa's spine. Turning her ice cold.

"Who is it?"

Vanessa began to shake.

"My ex. Lee," she whispered, barely managing to get the words out.

The man emerged from the shadows. He was slight and bald. Wiry and ratty looking. Alys noticed his bad teeth before she saw the thing in his hand. He was carrying a sawn-off shotgun. It looked like a farmer's gun with the barrels filed down short.

Quelling her panic as the situation began to sink in, Alys willed herself to think clearly. She had to do something. And fast.

Leaning back on the floor cushion she was sitting on, she stuck her hand backwards and discreetly found her slouch bag which was alongside her on the floor.

Fumbling inside, she found the rectangular shape of her phone and stuck her finger on it to unlock it.

"Surprised to see me, darlin'?"

While Lee's attention was directed on Vanessa on the sofa, she pulled the phone out unnoticed from her bag.

"Yes, a little," Vanessa answered cagily, recovering herself and giving him a stuck-on smile.

"You're looking good."

It was Alys' only chance.

She concealed the phone by her leg. Knowing it was on silent, she tapped her recent callers' list. Owen's number was at the top.

She tapped it and then slipped the phone behind her, slightly under the cushion obscured from view. Not knowing if he'd picked up the call or not.

Alys broke into their private conversation, talking loudly.

"So Vanessa. This is the guy you've told us about?"

The ratty man spun around and stared at her meanly.

Alys took a shaky breath as he hissed at her.

"And who the fuck are you?"

"I'm Alys. You must be Vanessa's ex, Lee. Nice to meet you. Or as we say in Wales, mae ganddo wn."

She said it slowly and loudly, praying that Owen could hear her.

"Shut the fuck up, bitch. Or it'll be your last words."

Alys sat stonily still. Her heart raced.

Lee switched his focus.

Alys could tell that he was twitchy.

"Nessa, I've come to take you home."

He might kill them, if he found the phone and saw that it was in call. Sliding her hand to the phone, she pushed the side button to switch it off and then slipped the phone under the cushion.

It had been her one and only chance. She'd told Owen in Welsh that Vanessa's ex was there and that he had a gun. All she could do now was pray to God that he'd heard her.

CHAPTER 28

---------*---------

Owen and Paul were on their own in the Lobster Pot, finishing off their drinks, when Alys had called.

What he heard next Owen couldn't quite believe.

He stuck the phone to speaker and put it in the middle of the table.

"Paul, Alys is speaking weird. Listen."

They heard muffled voices, including a man's and then Alys' again.

"*Fuck!* She's not making sense."

Paul strained to hear too.

"That was a man speaking?"

"Yeah, and I'm not sure, but I'm sure she said *he's got a gun*, in Welsh."

"Whatever she said, her voice didn't sound normal. Something's not right."

Owen called back but the phone went straight to answerphone. He tried again. Then one more time, not getting through.

Paul ran his hand over his head, trying to think. To join the dots. What was happening?

"Vanessa has a past. She ran away from some bad shit in London. And recently there's been strange things happening to her."

Does 'Exley' mean anything to you?" Owen asked. "I thought I heard Alys say Exley. It's not Welsh."

Paul shook his head.

"Exley? No."

His face dropped.

"Lee. It's her ex-husband. He musta got out of prison."

"Call the Police," Paul told Owen. "I'm going up there to see if they're alright."

Owen was in no state to disagree. He wasn't much use with his smashed leg, but there was no way either that he was sitting waiting around in the Lobster Pot while Alys was in trouble.

"I'm coming too. We'll call the Police on the way. Take my car."

Lee pointed the gun towards her and then the couch, motioning for Alys to move.

Slowly, she got up off the floor and edged towards Vanessa, sitting next to her on the sofa.

Would Lee kill them? Vanessa tried to gauge his mood. On balance, she decided he would. He was volatile. High, she suspected. And he was angry with her. He wanted to make her pay.

He could see that she'd moved on with her life while he'd been sitting in a prison cell. He had to be bitter about that.

"What do you want, Lee?"

She'd made her voice as calm as she could muster. Even though her pulse was racing out of control, and she could puke at any moment.

"I told you, I'm taking you home. Stop all this fuckin' nonsense you're doing and get you back to where you belong. With me."

Vanessa stared at him levelly.

"Then let's do it."

She kept her voice soft, trying to keep a lid on the voice in her head that was screaming for her to make a run for it.

"Let Alys go home, and I'll get my things together. Put that gun away. There's no need for that. I'll come quietly back to London with you. It'll be just you and me. Like old times, yeah?"

His eyes flicked between her and Alys. He was edgy as hell.

"No can do, Nessa. She's seen my face. She's a witness. She has to be eliminated."

Alys gasped as she heard him deliver her fate. Vanessa grabbed onto her hand and held it tightly.

"No," Alys uttered, trying not to panic. "I won't tell anyone. I promise."

"She won't tell," Vanessa agreed. "I can vouch for her. Lee, please let her go."

Alys whispered to her friend, "I don't want to leave you."

Vanessa squeezed her hand. It would be alright. She'd handle him.

Staring at his ex-wife, Lee seemed to be weighing things up for a second.

He waved the gun at Alys, motioning for her to get up.

"Thank you."

Slowly, Alys lifted herself off the sofa, releasing Vanessa's hand and putting both hands in the air for him to see. She stood facing him.

"Go on. Get the fuck outta here."

Alys started edging slowly towards him, keeping a distance between them and making sure she made no sudden movements.

She was now level with him.

"Stop."

She froze.

He pointed his gun at Vanessa.

"If any cops turn up, she gets it. And then, I'll come after you."

Alys looked terrified as he flung her a cruel stare.

His dilated pupils gave him an air of detachment that Vanessa had seen before. She'd say he was on crystal meth or some other class A concoction.

He turned on Alys.

"Well, go on then. Off ya pop. Fuck off."

Sliding slowly past him, her back now to him, Alys moved towards the darkness of the kitchen.

Suddenly in her peripheral vision, she caught a glimpse. A glimpse, that she would later realise saved her life.

What she saw was his arm lifting. He was raising the gun. To shoot her in the back.

She bolted. Diving for cover behind the kitchen island as the first bang went off. Vanessa screamed. The shot had smashed into a cupboard above Alys' head. It sent a spray of smashed shards of glass and crockery onto the floor.

Before he could shoot again, like lightning she scooted low and out of the back door. She leapt for cover around the side of the house as another deafening bang went off in the kitchen.

Running for her life, she sprinted across the drive to the shelter of Vanessa's SUV, slamming headfirst into the man hiding behind the front wheel arch.

"Paul!"

She ducked low and he held her as she started to shake.

"Alys. Thank God... You're safe. I heard the shots. What about V?"

"Two shots at me in the kitchen. He missed," she uttered, recovering.

"I'm going in there."

Paul suddenly fell silent as he saw Lee coming to the door. He put his hand over Alys' mouth and she sat with him deadly still behind the wheel of the truck.

Lee peered out into the darkness. He pulled two more cartridges out of his padded jacket pocket and snapped the barrel of the shotgun to reload it.

Scanning around, he fired two random shots into the darkness. One directly ahead of the door and another over the top of the SUV.

He reloaded again, then disappeared back into the house.

"Paul, it's not safe. He's dangerous. He's taken something. Wait for the police."

"In your opinion, might he kill her?"

Alys had no qualms in answering.

"Yes. He might. If he can't get what he wants."

That was enough for Paul.

Alys carried on.

"If she gets stroppy with him. His eyes are wild. If his temper snaps, he could lose it. But, Vanessa's handling him pretty well, Paul. She's been calm so far. Playing along. In fact, she was amazing."

Paul rubbed her shoulder as he got the information he needed.

Vanessa was in the living room sitting on the sofa. The kitchen light wasn't on. No, she didn't see a key in the back-door lock, but she hadn't had time to look properly.

"Owen's up the drive waiting for the police. Go now," he instructed her. "While he's not about."

"Be careful."

She pecked him on the cheek, then sprinted up the lane into the darkness.

As soon as Owen saw her, he clasped her tightly in his arms.

"I heard the shots. I was so worried. Are you alright? Did he hurt you?"

"I'm fine," Alys reassured him. "I had a lucky escape. Vanessa's still in there. The man's a psycho."

"The police are sending an armed response unit."

Alys began to panic.

"If he sees a blue light, he'll kill her. He said he'd go after me too. Owen, he tried to shoot me in the back."

Owen held her as she began to shake uncontrollably. The reality of her ordeal finally kicking in.

"Alys, phoning me was the bravest thing. You're safe now."

CHAPTER 29

---------*---------

P aul's military training kicked in. He eased his way swiftly
and smoothly towards the backdoor. Keeping low. Staying in the shadows.

The door that he thought Lee had shut behind him, was now
pulled ajar.

It could be a trap. Only when he was absolutely certain of Lee's
location would he go in.

His ears strained in the silence.

Nothing.

Creeping his way around the outside of the house, he crouched
under the living room window and peeped up, hoping to find a
crack in the curtains. They were shut tight. He couldn't see anything inside. But he could see shadows moving.

It was a risk. But, if Alys was correct, Vanessa was sitting on the
sofa. That meant that the moving shadow had to be Lee.

Paul moved soundlessly back towards the kitchen and inched
the door open a little more. Creeping low through the kitchen
darkness he avoided the glass and crockery shards that would
give his position away.

He found his first place of cover behind the kitchen island.
Squatting down, he waited soundlessly for his opportunity to
move towards the living room.

The police arrived while Paul was in the kitchen. They'd received Owen's message to keep away from the house and were parked a quarter of a mile back up the lane towards Freshwater Bay.

They'd brought an armed response team and there was an ambulance on standby. Two officers came up to Owen's car, and Alys explained the full situation.

"So, we've got an armed ex-husband, a female hostage, and a civilian playing hero in there too?" the senior officer confirmed.

Alys nodded.

"Just what we need," the officer said cynically.

"Paul was a para," Owen added.

The police officer sighed.

"Handy if we need someone to jump out of an aeroplane. I wish he'd have let us do our job."

"This Lee. Do either of you know anything about him?"

Alys shuddered.

"He's mean. He tried to shoot me twice after pretending to let me go. Think he's taken drugs. He looked wild."

"He's been in prison. Vanessa had moved away. That's all I know, Owen added. "And he thinks this guy's been stalking her. Hanging around, watching her. Someone keyed her car and vandalised a marquee. She's got a wedding business."

The police officer talked into his radio.

"We've got an IC1 male, armed and dangerous, possibly under the influence, ex con. He's holding an IC1 female hostage. I repeat he has a shotgun and has used it. Do not approach until directed. Do not approach. Inside the house, there's an unarmed IC3 male, ex-military, trying to play the hero. Over."

The policeman ushered Owen and Alys back behind the police line.

Armed officers got into position. Night-sights on, covering the two doors. Their next challenge was making contact with the hostage-taker.

In their experience, these domestics could drag on. And they could go either way. It was going to be a long night.

◆ ◆ ◆

Paul was now up, behind the door of the living room. Hiding in the shadows. Through the crack in the door he had a limited view of Vanessa. He couldn't see Lee. But he could hear everything. And the guy sounded hyperactive and erratic. Unpredictable. That wasn't good.

Listening to Vanessa, he hoped that she carried on playing along with him, being nice. If not? He agreed with Alys, Lee was likely to use that gun.

"What d'ya mean, you weren't happy? As I remember it, you couldn't get enough of me."

"You must be right," she said flatly. "I've forgotten."

He seemed to soften.

"Yes you have. But don't worry, Nessa I'll remind you later."

Paul's fists balled. If he touched one hair on V's head, he'd kill him.

"You used to be happy."

"Yes. If you say so," she uttered automatically.

"You were having a breakdown when you ran. Those skanks, they brainwashed you. Put you up to it. The Nessa I knew never wanted to go. They made you do it."

Paul heard him shuffle.

"We need to go. The car's outside."

For the first time, he came into view. He was standing at the sofa right by her now.

"Okay."

Paul could tell she was playing for time.

"Can I get my stuff?"

She was still rooted to the sofa.

"You don't need anything."

His voice was commanding. How far could she push him?

"I do. I need, you know, women's things," she hedged. "Some pads. And my toothbrush. A change of clothes."

Paul saw the sweet persuasive smile she gave him. Good girl, she was still trying to humour him.

"Let me go pack a small bag, Lee? It'll take seconds."

Now the puppy-dog eyes. She looked imploringly in the direction of the man who had now slipped out of Paul's vision.

"No. We're going now."

"Let me make a quick call, then. I've got a wedding tomorrow and I can't let them down, Lee."

She was trying again.

"Fuck the wedding. Let's go."

Paul bristled. The guy was getting more agitated. It was a dangerous moment for her. He had to get her out of there, but the distance was too far for him to spring him. If he ran from the doorway, he'd be shot instantly. An easy target.

"Lee, what if I say I wanna stay here? You could stay with me? Us together."

"You fuckin' laughing at me?"

He was shouting.

Paul could see Vanessa cowering back into the sofa. Scared.

"Think you can do what you want?"

Lee's mood was a hair-trigger between in-control hatred and out-of-control explosive anger. He was one dangerous son of a bitch.

"You can stay here, sweetheart, but you won't be putting up any more tents."

"Is that a threat, Lee?"

She was holding her chin up defiantly. Paul was worried.

Things were getting tetchy between them. She'd done the right thing. She'd gone along with his plans and she'd stalled him. But now, this defiant face he saw through the crack in the door, it was as if a switch had been flicked in Vanessa's head. She was starting to stand up to him.

Dammit. One spark and Lee could blow. He had to get in there before the controlling son of a bitch tried to put her back in her place.

Paul had one chance.

He was familiar with the layout. There was a sofa chair in front of the door he was concealed behind. He couldn't see it, but his only chance was to move to behind that chair and wait.

It wasn't a great option, as he'd only have limited cover and he had to hope that Lee didn't see him coming in. But it was all he had.

"Nessa, stop the bullshit. We're leaving. Now."

On the sound of his voice, hoping Lee was distracted, he made a break for it. Shifting from the door, he crept on the balls of his feet into the lounge, crouching in low behind the first chair.

"Please, Lee, let me put in that call. I'll get one of my team to put the marquee up. If there's a problem with the wedding, the police'll find out I'm missing. This'll buy us time. Come on, Lee. What d'you say? "

He'd made it. But he was vulnerable. If Lee moved back now, he'd see him. Vanessa spotted Paul creeping into the living room from the door as she talked to Lee. Without thought, her lips curved slightly, giving Paul's position away.

Paul could see how she quickly checked herself. She was trying to keep still and not look at the chair. She focussed on trying to give Lee the full attention he craved from her.

Luckily, Lee seemed to be buying it.

"You always were a stubborn one, Nessa. You're like the tiger I trained. So much harder to break than the lions. Even without their teeth."

The living room was eerily silent.

"How did you find me?"

Vanessa sensed the need to keep him talking. Distract him, help Paul make the next move.

"You used your mother's name. That, plus the circus name for your business. Oh and your photo on your webpage. It wasn't hard Nessa. In fact, it was piss easy. That's why you need me. You always were the pretty one. It was me with the smarts."

"Where d'ya want to take me? Back to the club? Is that it? You want me pole dancing, again?"

"And what was wrong with that, Nessa? You too good for that now? Are you turning your nose up at your old life? At me? You stuck up cow."

She threw him an arsey sneer that worried Paul. His mood was rapidly escalating out of control and she was struggling to keep a lid on her emotions and fears.

"I'm Vanessa now."

"No you're fucking not," he bellowed.

He raised the back of his free hand to her, and she instinctively flinched, slinking back into the sofa.

Paul got ready to pounce.

He didn't have a clear line. But, no way would he sit there and let him beat her.

"And don't look at me like you'd like to bust my balls. Or I'll have to knock you about a little so you'll start showing me some respect."

Out of the silence, something squealed from outside. It was high pitched and metallic, like a prison P.A. system.

"What the ff...kk?"

Lee twitched and spun around sharply, his eyes fixed on the curtains.

"Lee?"

A blurred metallic sounding male voice rang out from outside.

"Lee. This is South Wales Police. Pick up the phone."

Lee's eyes scoured the room in a frenzy.

"That Welsh bitch's called the police."

He raised his gun towards Vanessa.

"If I go. You go too."

Paul gritted his teeth, steeling himself to act. It had to be now.

Vanessa's phone rang out. The frivolous Mission Impossible ringtone that usually amused her, this time made her cringe.

Paul sank back. Lee was too edgy. He'd fire that gun and it was pointing straight at Vanessa. He willed himself to wait a little longer.

"My phone. It's over there. They want us to pick up."

The Mission Impossible ringtone started up again.

Vanessa pointed to the shelf above the hearth where her phone sat charging.

"Want me to get it?"

He nodded.

"Yeah. Shut it up."

Paul stuck his head out from behind the chair and nodded to her. It was a signal that he was about to attack.

Lee motioned for her to move and Vanessa slowly got up from the sofa and began walking over to the phone.

Paul took his chance. Springing swiftly from his cover at the back of the chair, he leaped on Lee from behind with full force. Jumping onto Lee's back, Paul twisted his neck violently, bringing him down hard onto his knees, then to the ground.

Paul moved his weight to overpower him. But Lee clung possessively to the shotgun, his hand gripping the trigger.

Seeing the struggle and Lee's hand on the gun, Vanessa dived around the back of the sofa, a split second before the gun burst into life.

Out of control, the gun banged and the cartridge exploded the stuffing out of the sofa's side.

Paul looked up in horror.

A large hole was blown out of the sofa. Exactly where Vanessa was hiding.

It was the moment of weakness Lee needed. Wrestling him, Lee fought back hard, trying to point the shortened barrels of the shotgun back towards Paul. He had one cartridge left in the chamber.

Rotating swiftly, Lee swung his arm back to point the gun, but Paul anticipating the move, grabbed the stubby barrel and began to violently wrench it from him.

The gun went off again.

This time crashing upwards and smashing the top of the lounge window.

The kick back loosened Lee's grip, and taking his chance Paul hurled the shotgun clear as Lee tried to move his hand up and gouge Paul's eyes out.

Paul blocked him. And grabbing his hand in defence, he threw Lee back, flinging his full weight onto him, overpowering him on the floor and finally wrestling him over onto his front.

Sticking his knee into Lee's back, he punched the side of the head before holding on to Lee's arms and pinning him down in an arm lock.

Lee's arms were fixed immovably behind his back.

Suddenly the place exploded.

A door smashed in. Followed by shouting. Piercing lights. Armed police officers stormed into the house, piling in behind each other, pointing their guns into the darkness of the kitchen and the front hallway. Within seconds they'd crowded into the lounge.

One officer swiftly took the shotgun off the floor and the others pointed their guns at Paul who reluctantly released his grip on Lee and placed his hands high in the air as he moved off him.

Familiar with the drill, Lee instantly complied. He spread his arms out wide, flat out on the floor.

"You. Get up."

A policeman barked at Paul as he slowly rose to a standing position. His hands now behind his head.

"Vanessa," he called out. "Officers, please. Check behind the sofa."

"Over there! Now!"

Paul couldn't get the words out.

He was forced by the armed policeman to leave the scene, whilst one another one rushed behind the sofa.

Assessing the casualty on the ground, they called for paramedic assistance.

Outside, Alys and Owen waited behind the police line.

From the end of the driveway, they heard the shots banging out, then the window smashing and finally the radio calling everyone into action as the officers entered.

Two paramedics were now rushing into the house with a

stretcher.

Owen held Alys tight. It didn't look good.

Paul emerged first. Hands on his head, he was marched clear of the house and then released to the waiting police who took him back with them to the main police line, where Alys and Owen were.

"Is Vanessa alright?"

Paul shrugged helplessly.

A couple of minutes later, Lee came out, cuffed. He was bundled into a police car.

He threw a mean look towards the police line as he drove past in the back of the vehicle.

Alys shivered.

Finally, a stretcher emerged from the front door and was loaded into the ambulance that was backed up now, near the house.

Paul ran forward and joined them, speeding off to the trauma unit.

The senior officer finally caught up with Owen and Alys. A police officer was driving them back to the Lobster Pot.

"She'll be alright," he confirmed. "They saw blood when they first checked her out. But we're pretty sure she was playing dead."

Alys sniffed.

"Thank God."

"She's got a gunshot graze to her foot," the officer continued. "The sofa saved her from most of the blast. Your mate Paul was a hero. Bloody stupid, mind. Trying to tackle an armed nutter, like that one. Domestics like this one, they don't usually end well."

CHAPTER 30

----------*----------

A lys initially tried to brush it off, but a few days of talking it through with Owen made her realise how lucky she'd been. Lee was back in prison and Vanessa was recovering at Paul's place.

She got straight back to work as soon as she could, and Beth and Gareth were now showing Alys and Owen around the rebuilt La Galloise restaurant. It was finished and ready to open for the summer season.

Downstairs was fitted out as a funky beach bar with mounted screens for sports matches. And there were high tables for groups of drinkers.

Upstairs, the modern restaurant was dominated by the big walls of windows that gave tremendous vistas of the clifftops, the sea and the islands that peppered the bay.

Patterned tiles created a vintage feel around the kitchen area, and there were two kitchens, as before, one in full view of the diners creating drama, and one behind for preparation and cleaning.

Beth showed them around, cooing and clucking like it was her third baby. Gareth followed them, hanging back with Owen, who was now free of the boot and the crutch, but still taking it slow.

Owen thought it was him with the silly walk, but today Gareth was limping like he'd pulled a muscle in his groin.

"Everything alright there, mate?"

"Uh... yeah. A gym injury. I'll be okay."

"Still on schedule for the move?"

"Should be. Beth's packing, so as you can imagine, it's a military operation. Don't worry, she's not breathed a word of it to Alys."

Now La Galloise was completed, Owen had pushed Gareth, and he'd got all the contractors working on finishing their home. The aim was for Owen and Alys to be moved into the boathouse for their wedding night.

Beth showed Alys the kitchen fitout. The proving oven immediately caught Alys' eye. It was a luxury piece of kit, but Beth explained how she wanted to bake her own baguettes, or 'beach bags' as she called them, for takeaways and casual dining in the bar.

Alys closed the oven door.

"Gareth alright?"

Beth regarded her suspiciously.

"Yeah, why?"

"He's walking like he's spent all day on a horse."

Beth made a snipping motion with her fingers. Then, put her index finger to her lips.

"Two's enough for our little family. After our last surprise, we're not taking any more chances."

Out of the blue, Alys hugged Beth hard.

"What was that for?"

"Oh, nothing," Alys gushed. "You took me back, that's all, to that night you turned up at my flat in London, after your ectopic pregnancy. I just remember how devastated you were 'cos you thought you'd never be a mum. And that Gareth didn't love you."

Beth laughed, biting her lip.

"I'm so glad we both saw sense."

"Me too."

After the tour, the four of them gathered around a window table in the restaurant. The future of Freshwater Bay's hostelries in their hands.

Beth was sure, she told them. She wanted to concentrate on La Galloise. With two small children, it made sense to refocus and take stock of what she wanted.

Gareth agreed. The months of running The Lobster Pot confirmed that neither of them wanted to be pub landlords. A restaurant with a bar was an entirely different business.

Owen waited until they'd finished.

He confirmed that he'd let Beth and Gareth surrender the lease as soon as La Galloise was open.

And then, they set out their plans for The Lobster Pot. Owen explained how it would be a boutique hotel, a retreat with planned activities focussed on wellbeing. Alys wanted to start a cookery school.

Beth was happy with that. Their hotel complemented the restaurant perfectly. Gareth thought it was an excellent plan too.

"And we're shutting the bar."

Owen studied their faces carefully.

"What? So, no locals drinking in The Lobster Pot?" Gareth replied, surprised.

"Only residents," Alys confirmed.

Beth looked at Gareth. They'd already built the new bar on the ground floor of La Galloise. They had nowhere to go with this. She sighed.

"Looks like I'll still be pulling pints, then."

"But we'll all muck in if you need a hand, Beth," Alys said, giving her a conciliatory shrug. "We're family."

"And I'm gonna need your services for the refurb," Owen added, looking at his brother.

"Yeah, no worries," Gareth agreed. "Should be finished at Rhys' place by August, as long as Ariana stops changing her mind and having more wacky ideas about what she wants."

Vanessa hopped into The Lobster Pot, her foot strapped up in an orthopaedic boot, crutches under her armpits.

"Hey!" Owen greeted her. "Nice to see I've started a fashion trend."

Alys and Paul, who'd finished their shift, joined them for a drink.

They hadn't all met up together since that night. Alys had covered to give Paul some time to be with Vanessa, and with hardly any time to go until the wedding, working double shifts had kept her calm. Owen had been taking care of all things wedding-related.

In the meantime, Lee's parole licence had been revoked. That meant that he was back behind bars for another couple of years, and the police were hopeful that he'd get ten years for attempted murder for his shots at Alys. Plus, there was the small matter of the illegal firearm and hostage-taking. Given Lee's track record, he was looking at being in prison for a very long time.

Vanessa could breathe easy again.

Paul had been floating an idea with her for a few days now. Planting the seed. Pouring some water on it. Letting it grow, and hopefully, flower. Last night she'd finally agreed.

"Paul and I are moving in together," she announced.

"Fantastic! Where? Your place?"

"No," Paul explained. "One of Gareth's eco-chalets has come free. We're going to rent it and get tenants for our places. It means we'll have a fresh start in a new place for all of us. Vanessa, me and Sam."

Owen went to the bar and came back with a bottle of bubbles and four flute glasses.

Popping the cork, he made a toast.

"To your new home."

"Paul and Vanessa."

Paul stood up.

"Can I also give a toast to Alys. If she hadn't been so brave and quick thinking, we'd never have known about Lee."

"Alys!"

Alys laughed.

"You learn some useful things in school. Like how to use your phone on the sneak."

Paul sat back down.

"Is Marcel arriving tomorrow?"

"Yes and Celine. Should be interesting. They're using La Galloise to prep the wedding food. The new kitchen's massive, but I'm not sure if even there is big enough for those two huge egos."

"The marquee'll be up Thursday."

This wedding idea was suddenly beginning to feel very real.

"Move your vehicle out of the fucking way, will you?" Jo shouted out of the window at the scruffy young man in a torn and dirty checked shirt.

Getting out of the Land Rover in front of her, he was now approaching her car.

With a thick dark beard and unkempt greasy hair that was far too long, Jo thought he was more gorilla than man.

Madog was losing his patience. His Land Rover was heavily loaded on the back with a full trailer of lambs that he was moving to the lower field.

It was meant to be a ten-minute job before he went to town. It would have been if it wasn't for her. He had suits to pick up and a haircut to get, ready for his brother's wedding the next day.

Instead, he was going to be stuck here for another half an hour probably, arguing the toss with this rude townie.

"Lady, if you can't reverse, you shouldn't be driving these lanes," he shouted at her as she sat in her car, like the bloody Queen.

"What did you say, Gorilla Boy?"

What had she called him? What was she? Twelve?

Madog stared at the loud-mouthed woman in mirror aviators who was now stepping aggressively out of her black Mercedes convertible.

With a tight black t-shirt and China red lips, she looked like something out of a fashion shoot.

But it didn't matter how well those jeans fitted the curve of her arse, the fact remained that she had to move that flashy car of hers out of the way so he could get through.

"Look, slip it back around the corner. There's a passing place back there. I can do it for you, if you can't reverse?"

She looked at him in horror as he held out his hand and offered to take her car keys.

Amused, Madog watched, as stepping back away from him, she skewered the spike of her stiletto into a pat of dried horse manure on the road.

It lifted with her as she stepped out of it.

"*Ugh!*" she cried out in disgust and scraped it off with her other shoe. "No way are you getting into my car. Not without it getting a full valet clean, after."

"Whatever, lady. I've got a load on, so you need to move it back."

Jo was getting fed up with this. With his thick Welsh accent and probably very limited IQ, did he even understand the English she was speaking?

She slowed herself down and enunciated carefully, slowly and forcefully for his benefit.

"I... am... not... reversing... my... Mercedes... If I get a scratch on this car, it will cost me at least a thousand pounds. *Do... you... understand... me?* One... *thousand...* pounds."

The young farmer sneered back at her as if he was dealing with an idiot.

"Well, what has in your head to bring that fancy thing up these lanes in the first place, if you couldn't drive it properly?"

Jo was exasperated.

"I know you've got a trailer stuck on the back of that thing you're driving. But that's your job. So, move it."

"But I'll be reversing back uphill with the weight."

She didn't understand. They were getting nowhere, and they'd been arguing for ten minutes already. So much for the haircut. At this rate, the suit hire shop would be shut too.

Throwing his arms up in the air in final protest, he stormed back to the Land Rover.

He revved up angrily, then reversed the trailer skilfully back up the hill, blindly navigating it around three corners. His clutch was smoking as he jammed his trailer into the space in front of a gate, giving enough room for the Mercedes to squeeze past.

She did so without a flicker of gratitude.

"Snooty, arrogant, stuck-up bitch."

"Hairy, ignorant, country bumpkin."

She was still chuntering about him as she pulled into the car park of The Lobster Pot Inn.

Ellen insisted on keeping some traditions and Owen agreed to stay at the farm, rather than with Alys, the night before the wedding.

Not that she saw much of him. The boys were busy moving Gareth into his new home and Owen into the boathouse. It was a surprise for Alys. Their wedding night would be their first night together in their new home.

Her big, tough son was a real romantic at heart.

She was all packed up for their trip Down Under. Even though she had mixed emotions about leaving Madog and Jake alone on the farm.

And although Owen had offered to help Madog out with some relief milking, Madog was going to have a shock at having to look after the farm and his little boy all on his own. He didn't realise the half of what David and Ellen did for him every day.

Alys was at The Lobster Pot, her final night as an unmarried woman. There were a few staying over with her, including her parents, her friend Jo and her old bosses, Marcel and Celine.

The two French chefs had been in the kitchens of La Galloise all day, cooking and bickering. Beth had tried to go over to help but she'd had short shrift from both of them. One thing they both agreed on though, was how amazing the new restaurant looked. They'd be sure to return, they told Beth.

Alys watched with amusement as they sat together at another table drinking the burgundy that Marcel had brought with him. They were wrapped up in an animated discussion, which some might have called an argument. But Alys knew better.

Jo joined Alys and Beth in the lounge bar. While the two had been reminiscing about their days together in London, Jo had been taking calls on her phone. She sat down now and tried to join in, but both of them noticed that Jo wasn't her usual bubbly self. She sat listening impassively, endlessly checking her messages.

Beth put her hand over Jo's phone.

"What's wrong?"

"Err.. nothing. Sorry, I'm tired... It's work."

She stared at them intently, then shook her head.

"*Bollocks!* No. It's everything. I can't go back."

"Why?"

"What's happened?"

"I had a call from a neighbour. My flat's been trashed."

"A burglary?"

Jo eyed them levelly.

"No. They found Mr Pickles hanging by a rope from the kitchen unit."

Jo let out an involuntary sob and Beth put her arm around her.

"Mr Pickles?" mouthed Alys soundlessly.

"The cat," Beth lipped in reply.

"Who'd do that?"

Jo blew her nose into a tissue Beth had found for her in her bag and tried to calm herself, dabbing the smudged make-up around her eyes.

"The Lupu gang, that's who. They're Romanian. Sorry."

Finding a compact mirror in her bag, she assessed the state of her eyes carefully, recovering her composure.

"It's what they do. Kill the pet as a warning. I know. I've been researching their activities for the last twelve months. And they've found out and they're telling me to back off. And I don't, they'll kill me. Like Mr Pickles."

She sobbed again.

"So, what are you gonna do?" Alys asked.

"I thought about slipping abroad. To France. But apparently, they've got links with the police there. I'm not sure who I can trust."

"Stay here," Beth said firmly.

Jo tried to read their faces.

"Would that be okay?"

"Yes, of course. But we're starting the refurb soon." Alys said, reaching in her bag to call Owen. "Hold on, I've got a better idea."

She was gone about ten minutes while she talked it all through on the phone with Owen.

He cleared it with Ellen, and of course Madog.

Finally, it was settled and Alys moved back to the table.

"I've got you a place to stay, but you'll have to work for your keep. You can stay there for as long as you want 'cos they're gonna need lots of help. D'ya want it?"

"Well, I guess so. I don't have much choice," Jo replied. "What is it?"

"Looking after the sweetest little boy. Doing the cooking, cleaning, washing; that sort of stuff. And maybe some farm work? Milking."

"Sounds easy enough," Jo responded.

"Great I'll call them back."

Alys squeezed her shoulder.

"You'll be safe here."

CHAPTER 31

----------✶----------

I t was a hot June morning when Owen and Alys stepped out of the town hall in Holyguard to the applause of their close family and friends.

Alys was wearing the beautiful curvy green dress that Ariana had chosen for her. As she told Owen, she couldn't have found anything better. And Owen looked rugged and handsome in a dark blue three-piece suit that brought out his bright blue eyes.

Beth and Jo threw petals over them as they came out onto the steps. And Alys' hands were filled with carved love-spoons, a Welsh wedding token for a love-filled life together.

Jo had hardly slept a wink. She'd spent all night fretting about her apartment and poor Mr Pickles. He was an innocent cat. It broke her heart. The men who'd done that were monsters.

She'd stirred the hornet's nest. But, she reasoned, being here was a good thing. It had been lucky that she was out of London when they broke in.

She had to lie low for a while, and where better than the backwaters of Wales? It would literally be her rural escape. Holed up in a farm, looking after a little boy. Helping out. Piece of cake.

Jo watched her friend coming out of the registry office. She'd never seen Alys look as happy as she was now. Owen adored her and he was no fool. She could tell that when they'd met in London. Alys had snagged herself a massive beefcake of a man with a sharp mind and a huge heart.

And Beth and Gareth. They suited each other too. She was practical and a little bit bossy. Gareth was deep, almost unfathomable, but kind-hearted and witty.

She didn't know the other two brothers. But, Owen's best man was his brother, Rhys. The other brother? She hadn't a clue who he was. Who she did recognise though, was the rude, hairy farmer lout from the day before.

She'd had a shock when she saw him. He was wearing a suit matching Gareth's. He'd tried to trim his thick dark beard back for the occasion. But his hair was still unfashionably long and scruffy. Even after he'd tried, unsuccessfully in her opinion, to slick it back with gel.

Their eyes slammed into each other and she turned away.

Beth came over to Jo with an older lady by her side. With her, was a small boy dressed smartly in a waistcoat and trousers, matching the suits that the other men were wearing.

"Jo, meet Ellen. Gareth's mother. From the farm," Beth said, introducing them.

Jo held her hand out. But Ellen dismissed that and pulled her into an embrace.

"And this is Jake."

The three-year-old stared up at Jo, his face turning pink and his lip wobbling.

"Urm... Hello, Jake. I'm Jo."

She bent down to him but ducked out of the way, hiding his face behind Ellen's skirts.

She was scaring the life out of him. It must be the shiny dress, she realised, or the red lipstick.

Uncertain of what to do next, she found the top of his head and patted it. Not a great move, but it was all she could do when he had his face buried in his grandmother's dress.

"You'd better come and stay with us tomorrow, love," Ellen offered. "So I can show you what's what, and you can spend some time getting to know Jake with me there with him."

So this was the little boy. Her stomach flipped. This was well and truly out of her comfort zone.

She'd spent the last few years avoiding small children at any cost. With most of her friends popping them out of nowhere these days, avoiding babies was getting to be quite a mission.

Then, the penny suddenly dropped.

If this was the boy in the matching suit, then the other brother must be...the father must be...

"And this is Madog who you'll be staying with."

Gorilla Boy.

What had she done in her life to get such a cruel twist of fate?

He was talking to Gareth. Beth tugged his arm and then pulled him around to introduce Jo.

And Jo didn't miss the sneering contempt in his eyes.

"We met yesterday."

He deigned to give her his attention for half a second, then turned back and carried on talking to Gareth.

Beth rounded on her.

"Jo? What happened yesterday?"

Jo shrugged. Why did Beth automatically think it was her?

"Ask him."

"I will. I've never seen Madog be rude to anybody. What did you do to wind him up?"

Gorilla Boy and his family hated her already. Beth immediately jumped down her throat. Forget the Romanian gang. What the blazes had she gotten herself into here?

Something about that snooty woman drew Madog's attention. His eyes kept being drawn back to her, even though he hated her.

Whether it was her shiny raven-coloured hair or her fiery red lipstick? He wasn't sure. Or, was it her silver shift dress and those impossibly long legs that made her look like a catwalk model? A bloody rude one.

And now, Gareth had told him that it was *her* who was going to be living with them over the next few weeks. It couldn't get any worse. This was going to be a total disaster.

She'd gotten his goat. Her haughty defiance. Her blunt gobbiness. He couldn't help it. She made him want to argue. To challenge her.

It was no good. They'd kill each other within a day.

Gareth laughed at him when he tried to explain his objections. He pleaded with him to get her a job in The Lobster Pot or La Galloise. Anything. Just keep her away from the farm.

Why did his brother keep going to Jo's defence? Surely, blood was thicker than water? Gareth liked Jo, and he wasn't having any of it. Suck it up, he told him, laughing like a loon. Having Jo around would do him good. And how else was he going to manage Jake and the farm?

He had a point, but it didn't make the situation any better.

What had he done letting Owen twist his arm, like that? If he'd have known that it was the snotty bitch who'd wrecked the clutch on his Land Rover and made him miss the barbers, he'd have put his foot down. It would have been a flat *NO!*

Then, to top it off, all evening his mother had been threatening him with a home haircut. He was still traumatised from the last one he had when he was eight. The time she'd used a bowl.

"What about that woman, then?" he asked his mother as he came to take Jake to the tent to sit down for the wedding dinner.

His mother was on his side. She was concerned too.

"Jake was scared of those red claws of hers. And she patted his head like a dog. She doesn't look like she's got a day's hard work in her. I give her a week. Tops."

Madog agreed.

Then, after he'd knocked back a couple of drinks, other ideas started hatching. Ones other than the idea of kissing her.

He'd spent all night watching her. Every few minutes she'd been checking her phone. Re-applying her lipstick. Tottering around on those ridiculously high heels of hers. Speaking fluent French with Alys' cheffy friends. Air-kissing people she was introduced to. Who did that around here?

Even if it was only a week, he'd teach her a lesson she'd never forget. Bring Miss Hoity-Toity down a peg or two. She was going to pay him back big time for that clutch.

He'd have her up before dawn. Cooking and cleaning up after him, doing the milking. Those red claws wouldn't last long, once they started scraping out the cow shit every morning.

The wedding party settled inside Vanessa's newest marquee, set up at the top of the beach by Gwen's cottage.

The inside of the tent was lined in rich, red Saharan fabrics. Berber rugs covered the floor and ornate metal caged lamps lit the space. Alys was in awe.

"Well, seeing as I was an Arabian prince, I thought I'd surprise you," Owen joked.

The opening of the tent gave a vista across the small cove to the sea. And inside was a huge, round table fully laid up and decorated with rich red and yellow roses from Gwen's garden.

Marcel and Celine joined the group, serving up huge platters of fruits de mer. It was followed by coq au vin, a special request from Owen.

Everyone laughed as the Morgan brothers, in turn, stood up to tell their riotous tales about Owen and to wish the couple the very best. Jo hadn't seen them all together before, and it was interesting to watch. Each brother was so different.

Gareth was sincere, offering brotherly advice, making Beth go red with his tips on a stress-free marriage. Rhys was hilarious. He could easily be a stand-up comedian. And Gorilla Boy? Madog was nervous as hell. Don't waste a moment of happiness together, he mumbled into the microphone before he hastily sat down.

Everyone went quiet. Talk about killing the mood.

Jo studied him as he ducked back to his seat and knocked back a drink. He seemed a little overcome. He bent over to his son, his head bowed from view for the longest time.

Saving the day, Celine appeared with the desserts. Her speciality; a Madagascan vanilla mille-feuille layered with slices of fresh strawberries.

The guests were still in the tent as the sun began to slip into the water beyond the cove.

Jars of candles were lit in and around the tent, and Rhys brought out his guitar.

Owen said something to Rhys, and he took Alys onto the beach.

"A Moondance," he whispered to her, as Rhys sang the Van Morrison lyrics.

"This is how it all began, Mrs Morgan," Owen said softly, holding Alys in his arms.

"Kiss me," she whispered. "I promise I won't slap you this time."

"I have no regrets that I kissed you, Alys," he murmured, leaning his head to brush her lips with his. "I'd say that we both got our just deserts."

ABOUT BOOK FOUR

The Freshwater Bay Series continues in Book Four:

The Rural Escape
Jo and Madog

Jo Mack's life is in danger.

She suspected it was when she began to get under their skin. Uncovering their sordid operations. The drugs. The laundering. The trafficking. The slaves.

They sent her a warning. Keep out of it. Or pay.

She needs help. And fast. A place to hide.

How hard can it be? Living on a farm. Looking after a small boy. Spending the summer in Wales by the sea, with the man who hated her from the first moment his eyes slammed into hers.

He's grieving and he's closed off. He's taken himself out of the game. A single father, single-handedly running the farm. Raising his boy.

A brash London journalist who barges her way into his life, uninvited? She's rude and she's ballsy. She challenges him. Fascinates him. Breathes life into him again, and brings trouble to his door.

It was meant to be a rural escape.

She's the last thing he wanted. But she's all he'll ever need.

Read The Rural Escape Here

Printed in Great Britain
by Amazon

60258166R00132